"So you're a programmer?" he mused. "If you don't mind my asking, you're not married or anything, are you?"

Taken off guard, Karaleen spit out "no" before she recognized the impertinence of the question.

"What about the hardware?" Jason went on as if she should think nothing of his previous question.

He was so . . . direct! And apparently he knew more about computers than she gave him credit for.

"Say, if you want a sales pitch you'll have to drop by the booth later and talk to a marketing person." Karaleen tried not to stare at his eyes. She marveled at the contrast between their soft light color—more hazel than brown—and his dark brown hair. "And that is where I should be right now. The exhibits opened fifteen minutes ago."

"Do you have to leave?" It was an appeal that she had to make herself resist.

"Yes. I do."

Her hand lay on the table beside her empty coffee cup. He inched his own near so that his fingers brushed her skin ever so lightly. She tensed and drew back, just out of reach.

"Yes," she repeated, trying to keep the tremor out of her voice, "I do have to leave."

KARALEEN

Mary Carpenter Reid

Serenade/Serenata
BOOKS
of the Zondervan Publishing House
Grand Rapids, Michigan

A Note From the Author:
I love to hear from my readers! You may correspond with me by writing:

> Mary Carpenter Reid
> 1415 Lake Drive, S.E.
> Grand Rapids, MI 49506

KARALEEN
Copyright © 1986 by Mary Carpenter Reid
Grand Rapids, Michigan

Serenade/Serenata is an imprint of Zondervan Publishing House,
1415 Lake Drive, S.E., Grand Rapids, Michigan 49506.

ISBN 0-310-47362-4

Printed in the United States of America

86 87 88 89 90 91 92 / 10 9 8 7 6 5 4 3 2 1

To Howard,
my personal *Computer Consultant*

CHAPTER 1

KARALEEN HAMMONDS FINGERED THE trigger of her tear gas canister. She had waited long enough inside her locked car. She pushed the car door open and stepped out on the deserted country road.

Keep alert, the officer who instructed the self-protection class had advised. Karaleen's dark brown eyes swept the road in both directions, across the endless grassy field to the east, and back over a flowing irrigation canal to an expanse of flat, freshly tilled furrows converging on the setting sun.

She hurried to the front of the maroon coupe and shoved its hood aloft. She stared at the mute engine.

Then, stealing into the quiet countryside came a faraway whine, the sound of a vehicle speeding down the road. Karaleen gripped the little tear gas canister. How tiny it felt.

With mixed feelings Karaleen watched a blur in the distance grow sharp and take form. She almost wished it would just race by, drive on to Agricity, wherever that was, and send back the police or a tow-truck. Any sort of official car would be more welcome than the unwashed pickup truck that approached. It slowed. It was going to stop.

If she lived through this, Harry Turf would have to answer to her; that is, if she didn't ruin his vocal chords when she got her hands around his neck. Sending her to a farmers' convention because the Vali-Turf Systems marketing team suddenly yelled for technical support was bad enough. But, he had shuffled her out of their Silicon Valley offices at noon with a decisive, "There'll be a ticket for tonight's banquet waiting for you." Never mind that it was short notice or that she would miss the next day's important design review meeting.

She had rushed home to her apartment, packed, and was soon headed east on the Interstate, trying to follow Harry's casual instructions: "Relax. It's only a couple of hours' drive. Take the first off-ramp after you hit Agricity and turn right. You can't miss it. You'll love the Agricity Motor Inn."

Well, she had missed something somewhere. And here she was, on a lonely road watching a stranger unwind his long, lean frame from a well-worn truck. The man was probably in his early thirties, a few years older than she. His features were rugged, his hair a rich brown, and his skin at home with the sun. He looked to be a man on the job, nearly as unwashed as his truck.

He approached slowly, pausing to inspect the back of her car as if memorizing her license number. "Trouble?"

Karaleen retreated, motioning to the engine, while keeping the hand with the tear gas canister concealed in the folds of her skirt. "It kept coughing after I turned off the freeway," she said. "I pumped the accelerator, but the more I did, the worse it ran."

He turned to the engine, not waiting for further details.

"I had been on the road for nearly two hours," she added "maybe two and a half—"

8

"Then you killed it?" the stranger broke in.

"Then it stalled," she corrected.

Keeping her distance, she watched the man's deft, sure hands, hands that knew their way around an engine. In the back of his pickup she could see what looked like machinery, a chainsaw, maybe. He was no doubt a farmer on his way to or from town.

Beyond the irrigation canal, a flat-bed truck squeaked its way along a narrow dirt roadway at the edge of the field. It stopped nearby. Karaleen was conscious of the deepening twilight. For the thousandth time, her fingers caressed the canister's trigger, and assured her that the little device was ready.

The man stood erect, blew at a stray lock of brown hair, and concluded, "Looks to me as if you have a clogged gasoline filter."

"How bad is that?"

"Not serious. But your car won't run without a new filter."

How could he stand there and claim it wasn't serious? "That sounds as serious as you can get," she said, speaking quickly. "I should be at the Agricity Motor Inn right now. I must have turned off the freeway too . . ." She caught herself at the momentary sharp glint in his dark eyes. Dumb! Why had she advertised where she was going?

"No problem," he said smoothly. "Agricity isn't far. We'll just run in to the nearest garage. They should have a filter in stock and be able to take care of you in a matter of minutes."

Karaleen froze. This truck jockey couldn't believe she would get into that truck with him.

She licked her lips. "Look Mr., ah, Mr. . . ."

"Bradley, Jason Bradley."

"Mr. Bradley—"

"And you're?"

She stammered. "K–Karaleen Hammonds."

"Now, a pretty girl like you," he smiled for the first

9

time, "shouldn't be wandering around out here by herself."

Karaleen winced. Condescending remarks like that had gone out a decade ago. She was acutely aware of his eyes surveying her softly tailored beige suit and its V-neck silk blouse, carefully chosen not only to compliment her dark eyes and her brown hair, but more importantly to fit the image of a Silicon Valley computer-oriented career woman. She fingered the buttons on the suit jacket, then blotted her palm on her skirt. It seemed warm for early spring, but then she was accustomed to the cool climate nearer the coast.

"Why, no telling when a big bad wolf might happen along," he continued.

This time she bristled openly, "How right you are!"

His smile evaporated into a look of surprise so transparent Karaleen could almost believe it was a look of hurt.

"I'll be glad to make it worth your while," she offered, "if you'll just find a garage and send someone out."

"Yes, ma'am!" The words rang through the air. With both hands, he slammed the car hood. Its reverberations blended into the echo of his boots as he stomped toward his pickup. He glanced back briefly, his attention again focused on the rear of her car.

What was so interesting about her license plate? Or, did this guy get a kick out of reading bumper stickers? Hers weren't remarkable. One proclaimed, *I brake for Koalas* and another had an outline of a dove and the words, *The Way*. Both had been on the car when she had bought it from a friend the year before.

Karaleen watched him reach for the truck's door handle. Just as she began to relax, she experienced a new wave of alarm to see him turn and stride back.

"I can't leave you out here alone," he said gravely.

10

"I'm fine," she protested. "Please, go on."

His attention suddenly broke away from her and focused on something beyond her shoulder. Forgetting to keep watch on this Jason Bradley, Karaleen turned to follow his gaze. With an apprehensive feeling, she noticed a group of men, farm workers, making their way toward the parked flatbed truck in the field across the canal.

Jason had moved near so that he was stationed between her and the men.

Uncertain whether the closeness of this stranger unnerved her, or if it was the sight of a dozen more, she cleared her throat and repeated, "I'm fine. I'll just wait in the car."

"No, you won't." He spoke firmly. He might have been a father laying down the law to a wayward child. He didn't touch her, but his look took hold with an iron grip.

Karaleen's eyes dropped first. She shook her head, unaccustomed to anyone, except Harry Turf—and he was her boss—ordering her around. Career women negotiated, they didn't capitulate.

"Thank you," she said icily. Who did he think he was anyway? "I'll be fine. *There!*"

She got her legs moving and scrambled in, locking the door. She snatched her purse from the floor to her lap. She smoothed her hair and, shoulders straight, sat back to wait in what she hoped indicated self-confidence. When her rear-view mirror reflected Jason finally climbing into his truck, she breathed a sigh of relief.

Just then, the scene across the canal, destroyed her momentary peace of mind. Not all the farm workers had mounted the flatbed truck. Three of them hung back, making gestures in her direction and pointing to the gravel road that led over the canal. A loud, unpleasant laugh rolled across the water.

In a microsecond decision, Karaleen jumped from

11

her car and ran toward Jason's truck as it came abreast. She waved frantically. Surely he could see her. But the truck rolled on. She ran after it, waving both arms in the air. Now, really frightened, Karaleen raced down the road, her tiny heels pounding the black asphalt, her ankles wobbling.

When she thought she could run no farther, the truck braked. Slowly it backed to where Karaleen stood holding her side and gasping for breath.

"Want a ride, lady?"

Karaleen was positive she detected a grin playing on the full mouth of Jason Bradley. There was a firm set to his jaw that may even have stifled a full-blown laugh.

Silently, she gathered what dignity she could and climbed into the truck. At her first opportunity, she slipped the tear gas canister into her purse.

At the garage, which Jason had no trouble finding, Karaleen remained sedately in the cab of the truck while he talked to the mechanic. He was so bent on handling things, let him!

After a few minutes, Jason opened the truck door for Karaleen, saying, "He can drive you back and fix your car, but he has to finish the lube job on that Olds. Shouldn't be more than half an hour."

It was the first time either had spoken since the ride to town began. Sighing inwardly at the further delay, Karaleen got out of the truck.

Jason shut the door and leaned against it. "I could wait around with you."

"Thank you. That won't be necessary," Karaleen said politely.

She extended her hand, and Jason accepted it, a pleased look crossing his face. They had touched only briefly before Jason stiffened. His firm handshake snapped open, and he rolled her hand over. The green bill she pressed into his palm might have been laced with thorns.

"Take it, please," Her voice waivered.

He dropped her hand as if he had discovered leprosy. "There's no need—"

"Please," she said. "I want you to have it." She tried to look away from his worn work clothes and the dirty truck. Why did this farmer make her so uncomfortable?

"No, ma'am."

What a stubborn streak he had. Pride or no pride, Karaleen Hammonds paid for her taxi service. In a lightning quick motion she reached to tuck the bill into the pocket of his plaid shirt.

With a movement almost as swift as her own, his rough warm hand captured her slender fingers. He squeezed them against his chest so tightly that Karaleen gasped and involuntarily bent her arm, twisting her body close to his. For an instant, as he bent his face over hers, she tried to read his look. Was it disgust? Perhaps disappointment, embarrassment? She was accustomed to dealing with men who fit the descriptions in interpersonal relationship seminars. This man did not.

Then, with a flick of his wrist, he freed her. Using his thumb and forefinger he gingerly plucked the bill from her trembling hand, folded it carefully, making smooth, sharp creases, and slipped it into his shirt pocket.

With something like a salute, he walked around to his side of the truck, got in, and drove away.

Karaleen watched him go. She shrugged off a feeling of remorse at her clumsiness. But, it was not so easy to shrug off the vague feeling of excitement that lingered long after the dusty pickup disappeared.

Later, when an exhausted Karaleen at last reached the Agricity Motor Inn, the banquet was long over. Checking in at the desk, she found a message from Harry. "Reinforcements on the way. Lester Peterson coming up from South County office tomorrow." Just how much in the way of sales and contacts did Harry expect from a convention of farmers that he would summon the renowned "whiz kid," the great problem-solver from Vali-Turf's branch office in Southern California?

A second message told Karaleen that Vali-Turf's hospitality suite was in Room 231. She should check in with the marketing people there. They were sure to be holding open house, even at this late hour.

The third message cancelled whatever thought she might have had of dropping in at the hospitality suite. It was an envelope containing a convention packet and a note which read, "Join the sales team for breakfast at 6:00 in the dining room." Six o'clock! *Oh, yes, when in Rome. . . .* Everyone in this farming region no doubt rose at the crack of dawn. She decided against leaving a wake-up call; she could picture lifting the telephone receiver and hearing a recorded rooster's crow. She would set the alarm on the small calculator she always carried.

Karaleen shifted her weight from one tired foot to another and forced herself to concentrate on the diagram the girl behind the desk handed her. Using a red pen, she had drawn arrows pointing the way to Karaleen's room. Tired as she was, Karaleen was impressed with the hotel's size. Even though it was only two stories, the complex covered a huge area.

The lobby was beautiful, modern and clean-cut, but warmed with rich woods and colorful carpeting, quite different from anything Karaleen had expected in this area. On the way to her room, she passed the brightly lit display windows of the hotel gift shop. The shop had closed for the evening, and Karaleen had neither the strength nor the inclination for window-shopping. But, her steps faltered as an item in the window caught her attention.

She couldn't take her eyes from it. It was a brown leather briefcase, the perfect size for her. But, even more important, it had the style and class befitting a Senior Programmer in Silicon Valley. A rich brown leather briefcase like that one could follow its owner right to the top.

Karaleen craned her neck to find the discreetly hidden price tag. She couldn't make it out, except to see that, of course, it was in the three-figure range.

Karaleen wound her way through corridors and soon opened the door to her room. She was greeted by luxury that equaled the best hotels. *What a waste*, she thought. *Right now, I'd be grateful for a cot in the hallway.*

Later, she sank into the king-size bed and turned out the lamp. As always, she said a brief prayer. Half asleep, a vision floated through her thoughts of a tall, ruggedly handsome man in an unwashed pickup truck. The truck seemed to gather speed on the lonely road. It was bearing down on a briefcase, a rich brown leather briefcase. She dashed in front of the speeding vehicle and snatched the briefcase from beneath the wheels. The truck roared on out of sight.

The next morning, Karaleen opened her eyes and, to her dismay, saw that it was nearly six-thirty. She must have set the alarm incorrectly.

She dressed as quickly as possible in a navy blue tailored suit. She knew ivory tones, beiges, and browns, especially a deep, chocolate brown like the color of her eyes, suited her coloring better. But she had bought this navy suit nearly two years before when she first came to Silicon Valley and, in her mad rush to pack, had grabbed it, thinking it would be good enough for a farmers' convention. She arranged the soft bow at the neck of a sparkling white blouse.

She checked her appearance in the full-length mirror in the lavish bath. The color didn't really matter, she decided. Her dark brown hair hung smooth and almost straight to just below her ears where it curled into a resilient full roll that complemented her rather small features without overpowering them. There was enough lift and natural curl so that her short bangs swirled becomingly above her dark eyes.

Karaleen inspected the contents of her portfolio, a large, suedelike envelope that her parents had given her on graduation day. They were so proud when their only daughter earned a degree in computer science. It was a nice portfolio, but after a year of working back home and two years in California, it was beginning to show wear.

At the entrance to the dining room, Karaleen hesitated. The Vali-Turf people would be having breakfast off in some corner, reviewing Monday's convention and planning today's strategy. Harry must be convinced there is money here, she decided, to have sent four men to work the convention, and then suddenly send her and, on top of that, bring in Lester Peterson. She had never met Peterson, but his brain was the talk of the home office.

On impulse, she turned from the dining room and entered the coffee shop, an open area defined by a decorative wooden and brick partition. Seated within its confines, it was possible to look out over an ever-changing scene in the motor inn's lobby.

Even though she wasn't hungry, she placed an order with the waitress. It would be a long day. Between the fiasco with her car and then oversleeping this morning, Karaleen knew she was certainly not at her best. Better to regroup and get her head together than to walk into a breakfast meeting that must be nearly finished.

She scanned the convention program. She would be working Vali-Turf's booth in the Exhibit Hall, but there might be some convention sessions of interest. She recognized the names of several speakers who happened to be from neighboring companies in Silicon Valley. Perhaps she should attend and see what the competition was doing.

Someone was standing at her table. Automatically she sat back and put down her coffee cup. "Yes, pl—" she began, expecting a coffee refill.

But, instead of the waitress, Karaleen looked up to find a towering masculine figure. It took a second glance to recognize her benefactor from the day before. The face was the same, but Jason Bradley was now neat and clean and dressed in brown slacks, a tan sport shirt, and deep gold cardigan sweater.

"Sorry, I'm fresh out of coffee," he smiled.

Karaleen wondered if some natural element in a farmer's diet produced such even white teeth.

"However," he continued, "I have something else for you." He waited expectantly.

Probably it was an illusion caused by tanned skin.

He tried again. "Would you mind very much if I shared your table?" With a sweep of his big hand, he called her attention to the line waiting at the entrance to the coffeeshop.

Recovering, Karaleen stammered, "No, of course not. You took me by surprise. I didn't expect to see you again." She hoped her stare had not been an obvious giveaway of the feelings she experienced at the transformation in his appearance. He had been attractive enough in his work clothes in a manly, rough sort of way, but now, dressed in what must be his town clothes, he was striking.

She busied herself straightening her papers and replacing them in her portfolio.

The waitress came over. "Hello, again," she flashed an appreciative look at Jason.

"Coffee, please," he said, "and maybe one of those rolls like the lady has."

Jason grinned sheepishly at Karaleen. "Okay, so I already ate one breakfast. A man gets hungry, walking by with all these good smells and good looking food, and—" he hesitated, as one unused to invoking such an obvious line "—and good looking women, right out here in the open."

17

Still ill at ease, Karaleen resorted to an old cliché. "Flattery will get you nowhere," she said, but it didn't come out as lightly as she wanted.

"I said I had something for you," he continued. "It's an apology, for yesterday. I wasn't on my best behavior. I don't know what got into me. I'm not always such a clod."

She admitted, "I'm afraid I wasn't Miss Congeniality."

He cleared his throat soberly. "No comment." After a moment of silence, he laughed softly, and so infectiously that she joined him.

"I owe you something, too," she said. "Thanks for helping me out."

"No problem." He buttered the roll set before him. "Now, tell me about yourself. Are you by any chance here for the agriculture show?"

"Well, I missed the first day and last night's banquet but, yes, I'll be here today and go home after the show closes tomorrow afternoon."

"Where's home?"

"Originally St. Louis, but now it's an apartment near San Francisco, in Silicon Valley."

"Oh, yes, the famous hotbed of high technology." He looked disappointed. "Then you're not here as a convention visitor?"

"More of an exhibitor. Vali-Turf."

"Are you some kind of a sales rep?"

"No, I'm not one of the marketing people. I'm just here to answer questions when they get down to the nitty-gritty of how our systems operate."

"Oh," Jason replied, "You know more about interfacing than about interacting?"

"You could say that." His terminology surprised her.

"Does Vali-Turf market hardware or is it strictly a software company?"

She wondered if he was merely tossing out terms,

or if he understood the difference between software and hardware. She decided to explain. "We concentrate on the software programs first to meet a customer's needs. Software programs are like sets of instructions that tell the computer what to do. We recommend packaged programs when the right ones are available. Otherwise, I—we write whatever custom programs the client needs for a complete system."

"So you're a programmer?" he mused. "If you don't mind my asking, you're not married or anything, are you?"

Taken off guard, Karaleen spit out "no" before she recognized the impertinence of the question.

"What about the hardware?" Jason went on as if she should think nothing of his slipping in a personal inquiry.

He was so . . . direct! And apparently, he knew more about computers than she gave him credit for.

"We market a microsystem of our own," she answered. "But if that isn't what's best for the customer, we recommend something else."

"What about support service and staff training?"

"Say, if you want a sales pitch, you'll have to drop by the booth later and talk to a marketing person." Karaleen tried not to stare at his eyes. She marveled at the contrast between their soft light color—more hazel than brown—and his dark brown hair. "And that is where I should be right now. The exhibits opened fifteen minutes ago."

"Do you have to leave?" It was an appeal that she had to make herself resist.

"Yes. I do."

Her hand lay on the table beside her empty coffee cup. He inched his own near, so that his fingers brushed her skin ever so lightly. She tensed and drew back, just out of reach.

"Yes," she repeated, trying to keep the tremor out of her voice, "I do have to leave."

19

She stood abruptly, sweeping up her portfolio. She slung her purse over her shoulder, snatched her bill, and hurried to the cashier. Without looking back, she walked quickly in the direction of the Exhibit Hall.

It seemed miles from the lobby, or perhaps she was only anxious to put distance between her and the disturbing Jason Bradley. She traversed halls and ramps, passing meeting rooms labeled with names plucked from California history. She glimpsed a spacious pool surrounded by a restful, landscaped terrace.

What was that man doing here anyway, besides eating a second breakfast—one that she couldn't help but believe was an excuse to spend time with her?

She ducked into the ladies' lounge and sat before a mirrored counter, trying to compose herself while she pretended to touch up her lipstick. She was not used to being upset by admirers, if that's what this man was. She had never lacked for male companionship, but there had been no real romance in her life. Time enough for that after her career was established.

She took a badge from her portfolio and ran her fingers over its shiny surface. *Exhibitor, Vali-Turf Systems, Karaleen Hammonds* it read. Karaleen sometimes admitted to herself that perhaps her career was already well established. Perhaps it was time to think about love.

But she would be careful. There was no room, for instance, for a farmer in her life. Now that she had a career, she wasn't about to toss it away. Opportunities for a senior programmer would be limited, even nonexistent, outside large urban areas. Back in Silicon Valley, many women managed to have both husbands and glamorous careers. Yes, Karaleen would chose someone whose lifestyle would be compatible with her own.

She pinned on the exhibitor's badge. Funny, she thought, when the letters were reflected in the mirror they didn't make sense.

20

The Exhibit Hall was large, but arranged in such a way that it had none of the barnlike qualities of many convention facilities. Vali-Turf Systems occupied a double booth in a central aisle, an exceptional spot for exposure to the crowds passing by.

Karaleen received a warm welcome from the marketing people and soon found herself in demand in a consulting capacity. The salesmen greeted visitors to the booth, supplying general answers and literature. But, when the inquiries reached a point beyond their technical knowledge, they introduced prospects to Karaleen. She was right at home answering questions about the details of operating systems and programming languages.

She began to see why Harry had put so much into this show. These people were talking big. Karaleen spent nearly an hour with a man interested in a huge dairy farm system that would calculate everything from the amount of vitamins in the cattle feed right up to employee payroll withholding tax.

At ten o'clock, Karaleen slipped away to sit in on a seminar. In the darkened meeting room, she watched slides, absorbing information for her own use and finding herself impressed by the speaker and by questions from the audience.

A new face was present when Karaleen returned to Vali-Turf's booth. The computer expert from South County had arrived.

Lester Peterson in no way resembled the stereotyped absent-minded, pencil-chewing genius that Karaleen had pictured. He wasn't even rumpled, although his thick blond hair was slightly tousled. His heavyset body was wrapped in muscle, and he looked as if he worked consistently to keep it that way. His greenish-blue eyes were set in a rather boyish face that made him look younger than the thirty-one years Karaleen knew him to be.

Lester came on strong. If ever he had been a shy

21

youngster holed up with equations while the other boys dated, it was not evident.

"At last, I get to meet the beauty queen of the north," he said, and hustled Karaleen right out of the booth before she could snap out a response. "Come on, it's time for lunch."

In the banquet room, Lester selected a centrally located table with two empty chairs facing away from the speaker's platform. He took the lead in introductions to the six other men and women who sat at the round table. Four were growers, and two were from the state university. Lester was at ease with all, so much so that Karaleen wondered why he hadn't gone strictly into marketing instead of bothering with computer science.

The lunch was a cut above the usual banquet-style meal, and Karaleen found she was quite hungry. Between the salad and main course, she glimpsed, at a nearby table, a gold sweater pulled taut over a set of wide shoulders. She looked away, and then sneaked a glance back until she had satisfied herself that the broad shoulders did not belong to anyone she knew.

As Lester resumed his conversation with her, she dismissed thoughts of Jason Bradley. There was no reason she would ever see him again; that notion was strangely comforting.

After lunch, Karaleen and Lester kept busy at the booth. On one occasion, a rice grower engaged them both in reviewing a particularly involved situation.

"You handle yourself very well," Lester commented after the man had moved on, "in every way."

"I trust that's a compliment on my professional expertise," she told him coolly. The idea of using feminine qualities to further her position with men clients was abhorrent to her. She changed the subject. "The dollar figures these growers use astound me."

"You know, agriculture is a top industry in California. Of course, it's made up of a lot of small growers,

22

in addition to the big guys. As a matter of fact, many of these people aren't growers at all; they're managers or staff members who work for the big growers," Lester said. "But, I'll take computers any day. There are too many variables in the ag business—weather, pests, labor, the market. One year, they're doing fine, and the next they're fighting for survival."

The booth was due to close at six. Karaleen could hardly wait. She decided to do something she had never done before. She would have her dinner sent upstairs to her room. Might as well. Even with that, her expense account report would be modest in comparison to that of the sales people.

She was making a mental note to stop at the gift shop and pick up a good paperback for reading in bed when a familiar voice near the aisle caught and held her attention.

She glanced over to find Lester and a salesman deep in conversation with a visitor to the booth, Jason Bradley. She turned away, pretending to sort a stack of business cards she had collected from prospective clients, and listened as the three men talked about computerizing a citrus operation.

Maybe she would leave early. She began to edge to the other side of the booth. She would make her excuse to the head of the team and slip out.

Common sense told her that further contact with Jason was playing with fire. So, he worked for a citrus grower? He hadn't even told her that he was attending the convention. Yes, she guessed that he probably did fit the part of a grove manager.

But, before Karaleen could escape, Jason turned as if he had eyes in the back of his head. "I've already talked with your Miss Hammonds."

Lester and the salesman propelled Jason to Karaleen. Pinned on his gold sweater, was a badge that identified Jason with AA-Bee Citrus.

As the neighboring exhibits began to close, Lester

suggested that Jason have dinner with him and Karaleen to continue their discussion. Karaleen's signals of distress were apparently lost on Lester.

Upstairs, Karaleen slammed the door to her room and thought of locking herself in for the night. She was furious at being manipulated into spending the evening with a man she wished to avoid. In addition to not wanting—no, not daring—to be with Jason Bradley, she seethed over the way Lester had engineered the whole affair. It was almost as if he wanted a dinner date himself. Or, did he sense a current between Jason and her and wish to put a prospective client in a favorable frame of mind? She loathed the idea of being used as bait. She was a Senior Programmer, not a sales person obligated to entertain clients.

She showered and changed into the only dress she had brought, a white wool with simple, flowing lines.

By the time Karaleen left her room, she had cooled off somewhat. Tomorrow afternoon she would be on her way back to Silicon Valley, never to see Jason Bradley again. And Lester would be on his way to South County. She smiled. The joke would be on Lester and the conniving salesman. Karaleen had seen Jason in his natural habitat: a dirty pickup. She didn't know what he had said to the eager salesman or to Lester, but she guessed that he wouldn't have the spare cash to purchase even the cables for one of Vali-Turf's elaborate computer systems. And how much authority he had to act for his employer was anyone's guess.

In the lobby Karaleen heard herself being paged. Upon taking the phone, she was greeted by a rapid explanation from Lester. Something had come up. He had to meet with another client, and she would have to entertain Mr. Bradley herself. Before she could protest, Lester hung up.

Karaleen gaped at the receiver. How had this happened? Now she was sure she was being used. She would fix that South County genius and those marketing creeps. She would just disappear. She slammed down the receiver and turned to go.

But it was too late. Jason Bradley was in the lobby, walking directly toward her.

CHAPTER 2

JASON GREETED KARALEEN and suggested that they wait for Lester in a glass-enclosed nook off the main lobby. Karaleen stammered, "Lester can't . . . something came up suddenly. He won't be joining us."

"Oh?" Jason seemed genuinely surprised. "I'm sorry about that."

Not half as sorry as I am, Karaleen thought. Aloud, she mocked, "Well, if having dinner with me is that bad . . ." she shrugged.

Jason's tan complexion took on a pinkish cast, as if he had blushed. "No, I didn't mean it that way."

Karaleen reassured him with a gentle laugh. "I know you didn't. Forgive me for teasing." "I just meant—"

She interrupted, "Seriously, perhaps you'd rather wait and meet with Lester tomorrow. There's no reason why we must have dinner together. If you have something else you'd rather—"

"Not at all," Jason exclaimed. "There happens to be an excellent reason why we should have dinner together." He looked at her intently. "I want to. There's nothing I'd rather do."

At that moment Karaleen decided she also wanted to keep their date. Why shouldn't she have a nice dinner with a handsome escort? Whatever games Lester might be playing didn't matter. She could still enjoy the evening. It was just a simple business dinner.

"Let's go," she invited.

But almost immediately her steps faltered. "I just remembered," she said. "I'm embarrassed to be so unprepared, but I left the arrangements to Lester. I haven't made any reservations."

"I know the perfect spot," Jason replied, walking Karaleen out to the parking lot. "I trust you won't mind riding in my truck again." Without waiting for a response, he motioned to her shoulder bag, and whispered confidentially, "You'll keep a cork on that lethal weapon in there, won't you?"

Before she could do anything more than stammer, and certainly before she could recover enough to suggest using her car, Jason ushered her into his pickup. It looked cleaner than the day before, and the truck bed was empty.

As Jason climbed in beside her, she noticed that he, too, appeared different. He wore a tie which appeared to be silk and a brown sport jacket made of fine quality suede. He was no doubt dressed up in honor of having dinner in town. Yes, thought Karaleen, he's not a Silicon Valley type, but any female would be proud to be seen with this dinner date.

The restaurant Jason chose was in a restored river front area. Karaleen didn't hear what he said to the hostess, but they were led past several large dining rooms to a smaller area and a table overlooking the river.

As Jason seated Karaleen, her eyes adjusted to the darkened room. Flickering candles in replicas of old-fashioned lanterns added to the lovely sight of reflected lights streaming across the water from the

27

opposite riverbank. The walls were constructed of lumber from rough wooden boxes. Stacks of barrels reaching into the darkness above provided a screening effect and the feeling of privacy. Here and there a cotton bale acted as a serving table. On the wooden dock outside the window stood packing crates. An anchor lay atop a thick coil of rope.

"It's a charming place," she said, "kind of rough and weatherbeaten." She gently touched the pink petals of a fresh flower on the table. "The only bit of softness is this beautiful rose."

Jason's eyes were on her. "I could give you an argument on that," he said.

Karaleen instinctively opened her mouth to rush on to another subject, but changed her mind. Instead, she acknowledged the compliment with a full smile. She had made up her mind to enjoy the evening. Why not accept Jason's remark graciously and let him enjoy himself, too?

Jason ate his steak and lobster as if conventions gave him a good appetite. She had chosen the specialty of the house, salmon, which proved delicious.

They lingered over coffee, talking with ease. Jason told Karaleen about Agricity and its history. Specifically, he related many details about the waterfront and its restoration.

"You're better than a tour guide," she commented.

"The Central Valley area means a lot to me. I want to keep its culture and history alive. Of course, I live down in the southern end of the valley, but it's all part of the same agricultural area, and I travel up here often."

"You haven't told me much about your actual work at . . . what is it? AA-Bee Citrus?"

"Who wants to talk shop on a night like this?" he countered.

"Even though it began as a business arrangement?"

They both laughed.

Later, when most of the tables in the room were empty, Karaleen said, "I hate for the evening to end," and to her surprise, she meant what she said. "But, it seems we're nearly the only ones left."

Jason signaled for the check. The waitress placed a tray on the table, an equal distance between the two diners. Without thinking, Karaleen reached for the tray. Vali-Turf Systems had invited Jason to dinner, and she would, of course, pay with her charge card.

But with a swift movement, Jason intercepted and grabbed her hand in midair. His grip was so unexpected that, in an automatic effort to pull free, Karaleen rocked the table. Over went the vase with the rose. Their hands locked, Jason and Karaleen stared at water gushing across the white tablecloth.

Just as the water spread to the edge of the table, dangerously near her wool dress, Karaleen jumped to her feet. "I'd appreciate it," she said through clenched teeth, "if you would let go of my hand."

He dropped it almost before the words were out of her mouth, rising from the table so fast that his chair clattered over backwards. He reached to steady the lantern with its flickering candle. He winced and jerked his hand away.

Karaleen didn't care that he had burned himself. She drew herself as tall as her five-foot five-inch stature would permit. "I was merely going to pay the bill," she said formally. "After all, you are here as my company's guest."

His reply could have been heard across the river. "I am not accustomed to a woman paying for my dinner."

Karaleen wanted to crawl behind the nearest bale of cotton. The few remaining diners stared. Several waitresses paused to watch them. "Today it is not uncommon for a businesswoman to entertain a client," she explained in a low, firm voice.

"No woman pays for my food."

Karaleen's voice rose to match his, "Why do you think the waitress put the tray in the middle?"

"Who cares?"

"At least the help in this one-horse town knows how to behave!" The moment the words were out, Karaleen regretted them. What a terrible thing to say.

Jason flung down several bills that Karaleen knew must be more than enough to pay for the dinner and a generous tip. He stalked out. She followed.

They walked along a boardwalk side by side. Silently, they passed quaint specialty shops, another restaurant, several antique stores. Before long Karaleen was completely lost. She knew they had wandered a great distance from where Jason's truck was parked. She had no choice but to accompany the brooding man.

At last he stopped. He put one foot atop a wall at the water's edge and leaned his elbow on his knee, staring out over the wide river. The water seemed almost motionless, but Karaleen knew the black, glistening surface concealed a powerful current. Waterfront noises seemed to be at rest; only gentle lapping sounds broke the still air.

When Jason spoke, his voice was strained. "I hope I didn't hurt your hand."

In an attack of guilt at her behavior, Karaleen stepped near Jason. She touched his arm. "I shouldn't have said those things."

An instant later, Jason had turned to face her with both hands on her shoulders. "It's just that I got carried away," he said anxiously. "I forgot you had anything to do with business. I pictured you as being my date, a real date." He moved closer. "Was I too far off base?"

Karaleen caught her breath. His hold on her shoulders was disturbing, impelling. This man, whom she hardly knew, was going to kiss her. She saw it in

30

the set of his square jaw and felt it in the tension between them. And even as she told herself it was the moonlight playing tricks with her emotions, she wanted to feel Jason Bradley's lips on hers.

Instead she found herself enveloped in a quick, crushing hug. His lips barely caressed her forehead before he released her. They turned back toward the restaurant, walking slowly, his arm draped casually over her shoulders.

By the time they drove into the motor inn's parking lot, they were seemingly at ease. At the door to Karaleen's room, Jason politely took her key and opened the door. He said grandly, "I want to thank you for a pleasant evening," adding an exaggerated, "Ms. Vali-Turf."

She laughed. "And you, Mr. AA-Bee Citrus, are most welcome."

"I'll be tied up tomorrow until noon," Jason said. "Okay if I come by your booth then?"

Karaleen felt her shoulders droop. With that simple question, the evening's spell was broken. In a few short hours she would have to leave and never see him again. It had to end, but at that moment, she almost wished it didn't. Not knowing how to explain that there could be no more starry moments, nor wanting to, she merely nodded.

Inside the room, she threw herself on the bed. *That was just a fun evening with a nice man,* she told herself. A brief, friendly interlude. *Lester Peterson should have been with us, where he belonged. That way it would have been truly a business dinner, and Jason wouldn't have gotten any fanciful ideas.*

The next morning Lester was so nice to her that she began to doubt her suspicion that he had made up the story about being needed with another client the night before. He insisted that she take a break with him. *Maybe I look tired, and he feels sorry for me,* she thought. She had hardly slept. They sat in the coffee shop, and Karaleen managed to finish a bowl of cereal, the first thing she had eaten that morning.

The only reference to the evening with Jason was Lester's question, "Everything go all right last night?"

"Fine," she answered.

"You know, I got to thinking that maybe I shouldn't have let you go with this Bradley guy. After all, none of us knows him."

One of us does, she thought.

"But," Lester continued, "I guess that comes with the trade and all that." He downed the last of his coffee. "He didn't try anything, did he?"

Karaleen gritted her teeth. First Lester dumped her into another man's lap, for whatever reason, and then seemed to act . . . well, almost protective.

She decided against telling him off. Lester might have jumped at the opportunity to use her, but he didn't seem the type to plan it. She summoned a wilting stare and answered Lester's question with a haughty, "Of course not."

"How did it look? Does he warrant anything more than the usual sales follow-up?"

Enjoying the chance to disprove the superbrain's original appraisal, she advised, "Don't waste your time."

However, squelching Lester's interest in Jason didn't solve the problem of her interest in him. Everywhere she looked, she saw Jason's tall frame. Every voice was—at first—his voice.

She left the Exhibit Hall and took a walk. She found herself in front of the hotel gift shop, staring at the leather briefcase. It was much too expensive. She turned away.

Back at the booth, she kept one nervous eye on the clock and the other on the people who filled the aisles. Several times, she thought she saw Jason threading his way through the crowd, and was torn between dashing to meet him and slinking away. In desperation, she told the sales manager that she had decided to leave the convention a few hours early, and requested, "If anyone asks for me, tell them I've gone home to Silicon Valley."

After checking out at the desk, Karaleen whipped into the lobby gift shop. It took only minutes to make her purchase. When Karaleen left the hotel, she carried her suitcase in one hand. In the other was a new brown leather briefcase.

At Vali-Turf's home office the next morning, Karaleen hurled herself into her work with renewed energy. It was good to be back in familiar territory. For her, Silicon Valley provided a source of vitality.

At eleven, the company's chief executive officer called. "Have lunch with me?"

"Sure, Harry. Conference room?" Harry's usual lunch invitation meant nibbling at a sandwich sent in from the local deli and, at the same time, chewing on a current company problem.

"Let's go somewhere."

Harry drove the way he operated his company . . . decisively, with care but minimal caution. Karaleen sat beside him, enjoying the luxury of a ride through the green hills that rolled up on either side of the modern highway. This is what she needed after her unsettling thoughts of the previous few days, a pat on the back from the boss to tell her she was still on track, still making the right decisions.

She gained further reassurance at Harry's choice of a restaurant. They entered a bustling outdoor cafe, which Karaleen knew was more suited to her palate than to Harry's meat and gravy tastes. They sat at a patio table, its fuchsia canvas umbrella shading them from the bright sun.

After Harry finished his roast beef sandwich and a fresh mushroom soup, he zeroed in on his reason for the lunch. "You made quite an impression at the convention."

33

Karaleen looked wary. "Oh?"

"Lester Peterson called me this morning. He thinks you're the best thing to come along since printed circuit boards."

She relaxed. "That's nice."

"In fact," Harry continued, "he's sure you're just the person he needs right now."

Karaleen swallowed a bite of her avocado and alfalfa sprout sandwich. The whole grain bread seemed to stick in her throat. "For what?" she managed.

"The work is stacking up down south—"

Karaleen broke in, trying to stop Harry before he came out with whatever wild idea he might have in that whirlwind mind of his. "I'm sure Lester Peterson is perfectly capable of handling any situation that comes his way."

"He only has two hands."

"Are you sure?"

"Huh?" Harry shot her a questioning look.

"Oh, I didn't mean it that way." Why did everyone think they had to watch out for her?

"Okay," Harry mumbled.

She winked at this man, who was all business at work and happily married at home. He seemed to have taken a special interest in Karaleen's welfare, and she had grown to consider him a sort of uncle.

"Look," he continued, "I know everyone seems to think Lester is some kind of magician. He is doing a great job for us in South County. He's one of the best when it comes to running a branch office and is tops in the technical end. But still, I keep tabs on what's going on."

Karaleen smiled, "I know."

It was his turn to wink at her. "They really are snowed. You could waltz in there and give them a hand—"

"Harry," she protested, "my job is here in Silicon Valley."

34

"Of course, it is," he soothed, "and you'll be back in no time."

"Harry . . ." her voice climbed, then trailed off helplessly.

"I've already arranged for your advance. And you're booked into the best hotel in the whole county for Sunday night." He took a final gulp of ice water and stood up. "Ready?"

She clutched her napkin, her mouth forming a soundless *no*, as Harry barged away through fuchsia umbrellas and pink tablecloths.

Karaleen spent Thursday afternoon in a daze, unable to reconcile herself to an extended assignment away from the home office. Here is where she belonged, at the center of Vali-Turf Systems. Nothing could convince her that a stretch at the South County office would enhance her career. She tried to see Harry again; he had gone for the day.

But, a good night's sleep and a great deal of rationalizing did wonders. Karaleen came to work the next morning and tackled the chore of making arrangements for an indefinite absence. She turned over short-term assignments to her immediate supervisor, and filed the long-term ones away to be completed after she returned.

Her supervisor's remark helped immensely, "I'll never forgive Lester Peterson for stealing you away. Hurry back."

Harry dropped by midafternoon with more encouragement. "Knock 'em dead."

It was almost five o'clock when she put down the phone, having called and canceled plans to attend a friend's party that night. She wrote instructions for the care and feeding of the dieffenbachia plant in her office. She stuffed a few last papers into her already-crammed gray suede portfolio, wondering once again why the leather briefcase was still at home with the store tags attached.

She locked her desk and said farewell to her co-workers. Walking out of the building, she admitted to herself that perhaps going to South County for a while wouldn't be so bad. After all, the company's miracle worker had specifically asked for her. How could that possibly harm her career?

And there was a fringe benefit. She would be able to spend time with Rosalie, a friend from college days. Rosalie worked for an aircraft company in South County. Since graduation, they had corresponded, and Rosalie squealed with pleasure when Karaleen called to announce the impending trip.

On Saturday, it was a race to pack and get her apartment in order. Karaleen had decided to drive down, since she had never been to southern California before, and going by car would be more like a sightseeing trip.

Driving south on Sunday, she was struck by the immensity of the state. To read a California map was one thing, but actually to experience the change of scenery as the miles flew past was another. In one day's drive, she traversed a route that included mountains, desert, ocean, farms, orchards, historic Spanish missions, and modern cities.

She found her way through South County's maze of freeways with less difficulty than she had feared. She entered the hotel room satisfied that she had made the trip without incident; in fact, she had rather enjoyed it.

Harry had made good on his promise of fine accommodations. At first sight, she told herself that she had better not get too used to such luxury. She was, after all, a working girl. The room was indeed spacious and beautifully appointed, although no better than the one at the Agricity Motor Inn.

Stop, she scolded herself. *Forget you ever set foot in Agricity.*

A bouquet of flowers rested on the table by the

sliding door that led to the outside balcony. First, she paid little attention, thinking it was an artificial arrangement, part of the room's decor. Then she noticed with pleasure that the flowers were fresh red and white carnations. She opened an envelope to find a card which read, "Welcome to South County. See you tomorrow." It was signed, "Lester."

"How friendly of the South County branch office," she mused aloud, twirling a red carnation between her fingers.

Below Lester's signature was scribbled in small letters, "Sleep well."

How very friendly, she whispered to herself, touching the soft red petals to her face.

The next morning, Karaleen became disoriented upon leaving the hotel parking lot and drove in the wrong direction. This false start, combined with morning rush hour traffic, caused her to arrive well after nine o'clock and decidedly flustered at the business office complex that housed Vali-Turf's southern branch.

"Mr. Peterson's expecting you," the receptionist told her.

"May I leave this with you?" Karaleen indicated the new brown leather briefcase.

At Lester's office, trying for a casual, confident manner, Karaleen tapped lightly on the open door. "You called, sir?"

Lester seemed genuinely pleased to see her, and kept her in his office for nearly an hour discussing the work situation in South County. He finished with, "So, you see how badly we need you. Now, let me show you around." As they left his office, he added confidentially, "I'll pick you up tonight at seven for dinner," not waiting for a response.

The tour of the facilities didn't take long. "We're crowded here," Lester said, "but we hope to rent more space in this complex the minute there's a vacancy."

"I just hope I can keep all of the names and faces straight," Karaleen said, worried. She concentrated on the engineers and programmers with whom she would have the most contact.

"Everyone will love you," Lester said.

They returned to his office. "Saved the best for last." He crossed his office to a closed door that Karaleen hadn't noticed before. Turning the knob and, keeping his eyes on her, he pushed the door open. "Here's your new home," he announced. "Hope you don't mind having an adjoining office," he added. "It can be convenient that way. Of course, you have your own door out to the hallway."

Karaleen took a few steps forward and stopped short. "It's a joke?" she asked.

Lester's face fell. "What's the . . . ?"

Karaleen's new office was crammed with a jumbled assortment of office machines, furniture, and boxes. The knife edge of a paper cutter stood at a threatening angle beside a pile of narrow strips of paper. A wastebasket had tipped over, scattering the remains of someone's lunch. From a paper cup a dirty brown stain flowed across the carpet.

Karaleen repressed a shiver.

Lester's manner told her this was indeed not a joke. She watched him stalk toward the receptionist. Their voices were low, but she thought the girl spoke of "Thelma." Karaleen could not remember meeting a Thelma.

At that moment, a tall, thin, woman with blondish-gray hair appeared. Lester hurried her into an office beyond the receptionist. Minutes later, Lester came back to where Karaleen waited, feeling very much out of place. He was calm enough on the surface, but Karaleen could sense an undercurrent of agitation.

"Just a mix-up," he explained. "Someone got his wires crossed and emptied all the cubbyholes in the wrong place."

He closed the door to what had become the office junkroom. "Until we get this fixed up, I hope you won't mind using one of the cubbyholes. It's a little further from my office, but it will be a temporary arrangement."

Setting up shop in a cramped space would not bother Karaleen. But she couldn't put down an unexplainable, disquieting feeling.

"Of course not," she answered politely.

"Come," Lester said, "here's someone you haven't met."

Thelma sat behind a large desk in a roomy office, one thin hand, heavy with diamonds, hovering over a calculator. Karaleen judged her to be in her late fifties, although Thelma had the typical brown, leathery skin of a long-time sun-bather, which made her look older. Her birdlike features were accented by oversized glasses rimmed with glinting designer frames.

"Thelma is our office manager," Lester said.

Just as Karaleen extended her right hand in greeting, the woman behind the desk reached for a file folder. Karaleen, to cover the futile gesture, quickly switched her hand over to clasp her own left arm, casually fingering the sleeve of her blouse. *Of course,* Karaleen thought, *she didn't notice my hand.*

"Ah, yes," Thelma said, "She's our temporary programmer."

"Senior Programmer," Lester corrected.

She looked Karaleen full in the face. Her eyes were the color of a cold, stormy ocean. "Yes," she said. "I've begun a file on her."

Inwardly Karaleen squirmed, but she must have been mistaken. This woman had no reason to snub her. "I'm looking forward to working in the South County office," she began. "Everyone seems so . . . so competent."

"We're quite busy here," Thelma said.

"And, speaking of busy," Lester said, "I have an appointment for lunch with a customer. You two will have to excuse me. Thelma, you'll take care of Karaleen, won't you?"

And he was gone, leaving Karaleen to follow Thelma into a tiny room, which Lester had aptly described as a cubbyhole.

Thelma deposited Karaleen there and then departed with a crisp remark, "I rarely take a lunch break."

CHAPTER 3

AT THE HOTEL THAT evening, Karaleen found that the bouquet of carnations that absolutely sang with life the night before had wilted during the day. She moved it away from the sunny window.

She felt a kinship with the flowers, wilted, and headed for the shower. Karaleen was unaccustomed to cold receptions such as the one she had received from the office manager. She hoped it was just Thelma's way. Despite Lester's small show of temper, the mix-up in office space was probably just that—a mix-up. *Don't read anything into this*, she told herself.

Karaleen donned a dark, full skirt and a short-sleeved white sweater with touches of pastel embroidery. It was still early. She would have time to call Rosalie before Lester arrived.

"When can we get together?" Karaleen asked after she and Rosalie had exchanged excited greetings over the telephone. "Tomorrow night?"

Rosalie hesitated. "I usually do something on Tuesday evenings."

41

"Big date?"

"Actually," Rosalie explained, "it's with a bunch of people. It's a Bible study." Then she added tentatively, "Maybe you'd like to come along?"

Taken by surprise, Karaleen answered quickly, "Oh, I don't think so. I'm doing enough studying right now on the job. New place, new projects."

"Maybe some other time," Rosalie suggested. "I don't work far from your office. Let's meet for lunch tomorrow."

"Love to," said Karaleen.

Lester proved to be a delightful host. Karaleen was amazed at the number of interests they had in common. She had a passion for musicals and was pleased when she found that Lester shared her enjoyment of show tunes.

"You couldn't have chosen a better place to come in the whole state. No, not in the whole world," she whispered as they sat in a darkened restaurant. A group of talented music students from a local college was winding up the floor show, an arrangement of popular show numbers. Shortly before these same performers had served as their waiters and waitresses.

"If you don't stop applauding, you'll never finish your dessert," Lester teased.

"Oh!" Happiness bubbled in her voice. "Listen to this next one. I love it."

Afterwards they walked beneath a clear evening sky to Lester's car.

"What a fun place," she told him. "Thank you so much."

"I should be thanking you," he said. "I don't know when I've had a nicer dinner."

And she felt he meant it.

On the way back to the hotel, the conversation turned to another subject close to their hearts. They talked with ease about technical developments, finding that each of them had questioned a certain article in the latest issue of a popular technical magazine. Lester filled Karaleen in on current local news in South County's computer industry.

As he left her in the hotel lobby, he asked, "Did you bring your grubbies down south?"

"Sure," she said. "Why?"

"Wear them tomorrow night, and bring a warm jacket."

"Okay. You know, Lester, this is really sweet of you," she said seriously, "but I don't expect you to entertain me."

"Be ready at six-thirty." He turned to go. "And don't eat first."

Karaleen slipped into bed contented. Some aspects of the South County branch office might have been disappointing, but the person in charge certainly took an interest in the employees.

It was an effort for Karaleen to be productive the next morning. The tiny table she was forced to use in her temporary office was a poor substitute for a desk. The only video terminal available to her rested on an old wooden desk in the hallway. Splinters from the battered legs snagged her hose, and she kept having to slide her chair forward to get clear of the traffic lane behind her. Light from a high window glared off the display screen, so that she left for her luncheon with Rosalie suffering from a headache.

They sat at a table in a nearby fast-food place, renewing their friendship. Rosalie, blonde and blue-eyed, looked radiant.

"You must be happy," Karaleen told her.

"More than I ever thought possible," Rosalie beamed. "I never imagined I'd find a guy as nice as Rick," she glanced proudly at the engagement ring she wore. "I can hardly wait for you to know him. You'll like him, Karaleen. He's considerate and smart and he's not lazy, and . . ." she blushed, "he's tender."

43

"Wait a minute," Karaleen laughed. "Where do I meet someone like him?"

"They don't come along often," Rosalie assured her, "but you know where I did meet him?"

"Where?"

"Now, don't laugh. I'll probably sound like your mother, but it's the honest truth. I met Rick one Sunday morning at church."

"You do sound like my mother."

"Told you."

"I used to go to church all the time," Karaleen said. "You know that. Remember the beautiful chapel at college?"

"Yes," Rosalie giggled. "Remember how we poked each other to keep awake?"

"And chewed gum without moving our jaws?"

Rosalie sobered. "Nobody has to jab me in the ribs now to keep me awake. Although, they might have to tie me up to keep me away."

Karaleen was thoughtful. "Big change, huh?"

"Sure is," Rosalie said. "Come to church with me?"

"Oh, I don't know," answered Karaleen, pushing bits of lettuce about on her tray with a plastic fork. "I've never found much there for me." She looked at her watch and jumped up. "Certainly not a dreamboat like you did," she called as she went to dump the lunch wrappings.

"You might find something more important," Rosalie promised as they parted.

Lester came to the hotel that evening wearing jeans and a knit shirt the color of his greenish-blue eyes. It was the first time Karaleen had seen him in anything except three-piece suits. He tossed a large envelope on the bed. "Here's the information on that accounts payable software I promised you."

"What's the matter? Think I need to sleep on it?" she quipped.

"Never can tell when inspiration might strike," he smiled. "Do you like fish?"

"Love it."

The succulent, ice-cold shrimp cocktails Lester bought at a serve-yourself place down by the ocean were delicious. They sat on the beach eating. A brisk breeze blew in over the water.

"I see why I needed my jacket." Her teeth were beginning to chatter. "But is this all we get to eat?"

"For now." Lester showed no sign of cold, even though he had left his sweatshirt in the car. "I'm going to show you what crazy southern Californians do in off-hours."

They began walking at a fast pace along the beach. Soon Lester was running circles around her. She laughed and began to jog. They kept it up for what seemed miles. She held her own, sometimes walking, sometimes running.

"Say, you're in pretty good shape." His look complimented more than her athletic prowess.

"Do you think we northerners have to stay in out of the rain *all* the time?" She refrained from saying that he also looked to be in good shape.

Lester took her to a pie shop for dessert and hot coffee. He commented on the cash register, "They should junk this antique thing, and call Vali-Turf in to modernize."

"Have genius. Will travel," Karaleen declared.

Lester swung his arm around her waist as they went out the door. "*Two* of them!" he corrected.

"Two geniuses? Or, is it genii?" she teased.

By the time they reached the hotel, Lester had concocted an imaginary business computer system for the pie shop. As Karaleen opened the door to her room, he remarked, "By the way, I really should point out a couple of things in that software package." He motioned to where it lay on the bed. "Mind if I come in for a few minutes? Might not see you first thing in the morning."

Karaleen had a fleeting notion to refuse. She was always careful not to let herself be placed in any situation that might be construed as compromising. Doing so would be especially unwise with another staff member. Lester was a fellow employee, and only that. Wasn't he?

She hesitated too long. Lester walked in and proceeded to spread the contents of the envelope on the small round table by the window.

"Nice room," he commented, and dug into a problem he had found in that particular program manual.

Karaleen thought he would never leave. She found it harder and harder to keep her eyes open. Finally, sitting in a chair next to his, her head dropped against his shoulder. She jerked awake. He slipped an arm around her and tipped her face toward his. After a moment, he chuckled, "And here, I thought you were as enthralled with page eighty-seven as I was."

Later Karaleen wondered if she had been dreaming. Or had Lester come very close to kissing her?

Wednesday evening, Karaleen drove to Rosalie's apartment down by the beach. She met Rosalie's roommate, who was an executive secretary like Rosalie. The roommate was packing, preparing for an upcoming move to another city, where she was taking a temporary job.

"Wish you were staying in this area longer," Rosalie told Karaleen. "You could move in with me for a while."

Thursday night, Karaleen and Lester ate in the hotel dining room and then worked at the table in Karaleen's room until late. At nearly midnight, the telephone rang, and Lester automatically grabbed it. There was no response from the other end, and he replaced the receiver. "Well, you know what they say. If a man answers, hang up."

"Go home, Lester," she told him. What good was a

luxurious hotel room if most of your waking hours in it were spent working?

Karaleen was tired when she arrived at the office Friday morning. She was beginning to feel the strain of the previous busy weeks. And this would be another hectic day. She had promised Lester that a new version of a software program for an auto parts store would be finished by two o'clock that afternoon.

Sorting and stacking the growing piles of paperwork on the wobbly table that passed as her desk, she longed for her own comfortable office back in Silicon Valley. How could anyone be efficient in surroundings such as these? A heavy folder with the program's latest printout slid from a precarious pile onto the floor.

As Karaleen retrieved it, her telephone rang with an in-house call.

"This is Karaleen," she answered.

Without benefit of preliminary remarks, a clipped voice announced, "Weekly expense reports are due before noon."

Karaleen wondered why Thelma hadn't poked her head around the corner to tell her that. "I'll try, but it may have to wait until after two o'clock. I have to—"

"Is this your first expense report with the company?"

Karaleen gasped at Thelma's abruptness. The office manager knew very well Karaleen would have submitted numerous expense accounts. "No."

"The company policy manual states that employees will turn in expenses no later than noon each Friday."

Karaleen shuddered. *You're all heart, Thelma,* she said to herself. The home office treated that noon deadline as a goal, to ensure the reports were in before closing Friday so the finance department could have them Monday morning. Aloud, she tried to sound cheery. She wasn't going to let this woman's gruffness rub off on her. "Do my best." And she hung up.

Karaleen dug an envelope of receipts and a pad of expense report forms out of her briefcase. She hated to take the time she so badly needed between then and two clock, but she would cooperate and go along with the way things were run down here. *I'm just glad I don't work for her,* she thought.

A little later, she stopped in Thelma's office to leave the expense report. Thelma was out. How spacious and pleasant her office was. Thelma surely didn't get her grumpiness from her surroundings. *Oh, well,* Karaleen thought, *I'm certain her attitude isn't personal.* She had seen others recoil at the hands of this blunt woman.

Karaleen buried herself in her work, trying feverishly to get the job done. She would have to work right through lunch.

Sometime later, her head bowed over her table, Karaleen's concentration was broken by a piece of paper thrust unceremoniously on top of the tablet she was studying. She jerked to attention, already knowing, from the diamond rings on the hand that held the paper, who was standing over her.

Perhaps it was a refusal to believe such rudeness, that enabled Karaleen to ignore it, but she calmly put her pencil down and leaned back, saying, "May I help you, Thelma?"

"I'm afraid we can't accept this expense report."

Karaleen thought perhaps she hadn't heard correctly. She fought to keep her temper under control, not trusting herself to speak.

Thelma went on. "You failed to use the proper form."

Karaleen almost sighed with relief. At least Thelma had not taken it upon herself to approve or disapprove the actual expenses. There was just some mix-up about the form.

"That's the form we always use in the home office," Karaleen said. The moment the words were out, she wished she hadn't put it quite that way. It might sound uppity or something. To make amends, she said, "I'll copy it on whatever form you want later this afternoon."

"Hmm." Thelma, still grasping the expense report, tapped it gently on Karaleen's tablet. "Then, it will be late, won't it?"

Karaleen wanted to blurt out that it wouldn't be late if the correct form had been provided in the first place, or even if Thelma hadn't waited until fifteen minutes before noon to call the situation to her attention.

But she gritted her teeth and told herself, *I am a career woman, but I am also a lady.* She looked straight at Thelma and replied, "I suppose it will."

Thelma, seeming oddly undisturbed, left without a word.

Karaleen moved out to the hallway and signed on at the terminal. She tried to get her mind on her work, but it was hard. Her fingers wouldn't obey. Even the computer seemed sluggish.

On impulse she went back to her cubbyhole and picked up the phone. She had to call north for one last bit of information before she could finish the software program. She got what she needed and then asked to be switched to Harry's office.

They made small talk for a few minutes. Then Harry said, "Everything's okay, huh?"

Karaleen hesitated so long that Harry demanded, "Well, is it?"

"Sure, Harry," she said quickly. "Just wanted to say hello as long as I was calling." Then she added, "You didn't sell my desk, or anything, did you?"

"Well, I tried, but you know how things go. With the economy the shape it's in, I couldn't get cash for it." Sometimes Harry sounded dreadfully serious when he was teasing. "Oh, some troublemaker made an offer. I told him I'd keep the troublemaker I had."

Karaleen went back to work. She heard others return from lunch. It was a little after one o'clock. Less than an hour to finish.

Lester appeared and put half a sandwich on her table. "Share my lunch?" he asked.

Gratefully she responded, "Love to, just as soon as I get this program done. I'm almost there."

They didn't see much of each other during the day. In fact, this was one of the few times he had been down to where she worked. She would like to bring up the matter of moving her office. But she had no time for that now.

And it wasn't like him to waste precious moments. Must be something important. Maybe the details of the move were all arranged, and he had come to tell her. She looked at him inquiringly.

He cleared his throat and pulled a paper from his back pocket. "How about checking this over and signing it?"

"Now?"

"Why not?"

"You know why not, Lester. The same reason we stayed up until all hours of the night. The program for the auto parts man."

"How are you coming on it?"

She turned to her work. "I've about got it licked. At two o'clock, you'd better stand back, because I'll be charging into that meeting."

"Great. But, here," he smoothed out the paper and offered it, "this will just take a second."

Karaleen looked in disbelief at what Lester held in his hand. It was an expense account form, only slightly different from the kind the home office used. Her name was at the top. Her eyes scanned on down. There were the figures she had put on her expense report, but now, they were neatly printed on this form. "Who. . .what. . . ?"

Lester shrugged. "One of the girls copied it. I'm sure it's correct."

A sickening realization came over Karaleen. Thelma had gone to Lester and, like a child, had reported on her! This was ridiculous. That sort of thing went on in schoolyards, not offices.

She refused to dignify such petty tactics even by defending herself to Lester. She stubbornly resisted. "How about I look at it after I finish the job?"

Lester sat on the edge of the table. It creaked. He stood up quickly. "I know it's a little thing, and she's a first class pain, but let's humor her. She runs this office efficiently, just like clockwork, and it shows. She makes us look good." He smiled wistfully and added, "Just sign it."

Karaleen had to fight away sudden tears. She wrote her name blindly, then turned around, pretending to look for something on a cluttered bookcase. Lester was wrong. It wasn't a little thing at all.

"Thanks," he said, and she heard his pause at the doorway. "What are you doing still here in this cubbyhole?"

She was glad he didn't wait for an answer because, if he had, she either would have surrendered to a crying fit or thrown something at him.

Somehow Karaleen finished the auto parts store software program and took it in to Lester's office shortly after two o'clock. She felt like a mannequin posed on a chair. Her input to the meeting was limited to answering direct questions until Lester, with raised eyebrows, said, "Ms. Hammonds did the final work on this. I think she's the one to review the new inventory module."

As the meeting broke up, Karaleen slipped away. Lester had not mentioned dinner, but right then, she had no desire to see more of him. She drove to the hotel, beating the rush hour traffic. She ran a tub of hot water, and climbed in, determined to soak away the unpleasantness of the day. She wished she could pack her car and head back where she belonged, Silicon Valley.

Maybe it's the smog, she told herself. *It's solidified Thelma's heart. And Lester's brain probably runs on smog. That's why he's so brilliant—about some things.* She thought of Rosalie. Nothing had hardened her heart. She seemed so content. . .so peaceful. . . .

Karaleen had just dried and powdered when she heard a knock at the door. Hurriedly she pulled on a bright yellow chenille robe and shook out her hair. She opened the door a crack and found Lester.

"You left work early." It wasn't an accusation, just a statement. "I don't blame you. You had a rough day."

Karaleen wasn't sure how she felt about finding Lester there.

"Aren't you going to ask me in?"

Usually he just walked in without invitation.

"I'm not dressed."

"I'll just wait while you throw something on," he said and then walked in.

She disappeared into the dressing room and came out a few minutes later in a floor-length, dark green velvet dress, so dark it looked almost black. She had made it years before as a robe, but she felt so elegant when she wore it that she saved it for lounging. It had a deep V neckline and long full sleeves caught at the wrist with tiny jet black buttons. A black satin cord belt encircled the fitted waistline.

Lester had removed his coat and thrown it over the back of a chair. He saw her now and gave a long, low whistle. "You're beautiful."

Karaleen was taken aback. Lester never minced words, but neither had he ever said anything that personal.

But she was not yet ready to forgive and forget his part in the day's soap opera. She went to the sliding glass door and opened the drapes.

Her room was on the fifth floor. Below the balcony spread busy South County on a Friday evening. In the early darkness, pale headlights directed cars along the crowded streets. Nearby a faint wall of trees, manicured into ghostly round balls, outlined a shopping center that supposedly rivaled any in the world, and on every side of it were more shops. Here and there a group of tall edifices sprang from the miles of low buildings and leaned together as if in support. A jet moved silently above.

She felt Lester's presence behind her. "I can't get over the contrast," she said, "all of this is new and modern, always growing, changing, almost make-believe. And out there," she pointed to where the ocean lay flat and silvery on the horizon, "the ocean is so real, and it's been there forever." She stopped, at a loss to express herself.

She leaned against the balcony railing. Lester walked over beside her. He pointed to a large building under construction. "We should be grateful for some changes," he said. "When that's finished it will be one of the finest hospitals in the state."

Karaleen smiled ruefully, "Oh, don't get me wrong, I'm all for putting man's capabilities to the best use. I wouldn't be in the computer industry if I weren't."

"It's exciting, isn't it," said Lester, "to be on the cutting edge of technology?"

"You sound like an ad slick for a microprocessor," Karaleen chided. Then she returned to her reflective mood. "It isn't the technology race that wears you down. It's the people race."

Lester stepped nearer. "You may accuse me of speaking in advertising jargon, but that's better than sounding forlorn." He slipped an arm gently around her waist and pulled her close. "You did have a rough day, didn't you?"

Resentment welled up again, and Karaleen tensed, but she didn't move. Resting in the circle of Lester's arm was pleasant.

Together they watched the scene about them grow

darker and darker. Its muted forms mingled and faded, to be replaced by a jumble of tiny lights.

A self-conscious feeling came over Karaleen, and even though she was reluctant to break away, she ducked from Lester's arm, saying, "That's the longest I've seen you still, Lester. You're not in your usual *jump on it* mode."

He laughed, "Know what? It's your fault. You made me stop and think."

"About racing through life?"

"Perhaps a little." He sobered and put his hands on Karaleen's shoulders. "You made me think that maybe I'm missing something in that race. Like maybe a partner."

Karaleen caught her breath. She fastened her eyes on Lester's white shirt, tracing the white stitching of the designer's logo on the pocket.

She wasn't ready for this. She searched frantically for something to stop Lester from going on. "Partner, huh?" Her voice climbed and then fell back into a lighthearted banter. "Does Harry know you're starting your own company? Or were you planning on joining him in a kind of co-presidency?"

For a brief instant, Lester's expression registered something like shock. Then, despite the silliness of her remarks, he picked up on them. "No, I'm biding my time, waiting for the right partner. Harry's too far away from the technical end now. Besides, he's not pretty."

With that, Lester dropped his hands. "What say I order up something light? We'll eat out on the balcony."

"Are you inviting yourself to dinner?"

"That I am."

The order came quickly. Lester carried the tray to the glass-topped table on the balcony. He took the cover from a tray of fresh fruit, put it upside down on the table, and twirled it around and around, like a top.

Casually he mentioned, "Did I tell you I'd be gone tomorrow?"

Karaleen tore open a package of crackers. "Oh?" She had understood the South County branch worked nearly every Saturday because of its heavy load.

"Yes," Lester said, "Going to close up shop tomorrow. As a matter of fact, I have to be on my way shortly. I'm going down the coast a few miles. An old buddy of mine is taking his boat on its maiden voyage. He asked me to help."

"Sounds like fun."

"Actually I hate boats."

"Why are you going?"

"This guy is more than a buddy. He's got a little business down there. I think he could use Vali-Turf to good advantage."

"So you're going to sell him?"

"Why not?"

"It's fine with me," she said. "I can use a two-day weekend." Mentally she began to plan. Sleep late, call Rosalie, walk on the beach, explore that shopping center. . .

Her thoughts were interrupted. She shook her head. What was Lester saying?

"—since you were already gone, I told him I'd bring the stuff over to you. I said I knew you could have it ready for him early Monday morning."

"What are you talking about?"

"Well, the auto parts man was pleased with what you did. You left before he could tell you, you know," Lester shook a reproving finger "He only wants one change, but he needs it right away."

"Oh, Lester, I worked so hard to meet his spec, and now he's going to change it?"

"This won't be a big problem for you, believe me. But I don't like the idea of you working alone in the office. So, I took care of that." His face wore a pleased look. "I've got a terminal down in the car.

55

With a telephone modem, you can work here at the hotel. I'm going to get the guy at the desk to send up a cart with wheels. You can even roll it out on the balcony if you want."

Before Karaleen could digest Lester's plans for her weekend, he was out the door.

Mechanically, she tidied the table on the balcony and put the tray of dirty dishes in the hallway to be picked up. She wandered aimlessly around the room, stopping to leaf through a book on the nightstand.

Soon Lester was back with a box of papers. A hotel employee followed, wheeling a cart with a computer terminal. They set it up, and Lester saw to it that all was in working order. The hotel man cautioned her not to trip over the wires on the floor and excused himself.

Minutes later Lester left again, having first given Karaleen a quick, one-arm hug, saying, "You know, we make a great team."

Karaleen sat on the edge of the bed, her spirits drooped. There was no doubt about it. She felt abandoned.

But she wanted to kick herself for acting like a baby. Of course Vali-Turf wasn't paying for this beautiful hotel room and her other expenses in order for her to spend Saturdays shopping.

I'm upset being in a strange place, she told herself. *New faces, and . . . I'm tired . . . and . . . The tears came.*

An hour or so later Karaleen roused from a fitful sleep. She splashed cold water on her eyes and patted her face dry. "You've had your little cry," she addressed herself in the mirror. "Now, shape up!"

She dusted powder over her face. Her features were too delicate. She wished her cheekbones were more prominent. That might give her a stronger, more commanding appearance. She sighed. Looking younger and more vulnerable than her twenty-seven years could be a handicap in career advancement, so she did the best she could with make-up and clothes, and worked at developing her personality into a reasonable combination of a modern lady and a determined upwardly mobile career woman.

She combed her hair. She tried pulling the bangs straight back. Then she let them fall naturally and swept the longer hair back and up, turning sideways to see the effect.

"You're not beautiful, no matter what Lester says," she admonished the face in the mirror. Still, his was a pleasing compliment. "Maybe I was too hard on Lester. After all, he's working, too. And," she smiled slyly, "who knows? Years down the line . . . I mean, our careers are certainly compatible. We'd always have something in common."

The next morning, Karaleen opened one eye, saw the blank screen of the computer terminal across the room and groaned. She turned on the TV and watched a broadcast of dismal news, which she then felt a need to counteract, so she put on the dark green velvet gown.

Once she logged on to the computer and involved herself in the project for the auto parts man, however, she forgot everything else until hunger pangs reminded her it was late morning and she had had nothing to eat since the evening before. She ordered brunch from room service and went back to work.

Karaleen signed for the order. Only after the waiter left, did she realize that an error had been made. The restaurant had sent up brunch for two, perhaps confusing this morning's order with the supper delivered the night before for her and Lester. She indulged in a whimsical wish that Lester could be there to share this, too, when she was surprised by a knock at the door. Had Lester come back?

In mounting excitement she patted at her hair and smoothed her long skirt. With a quick step, she hurried to open the door, only to retreat in confusion, conscious that her welcoming smile faded into astonishment and that her knees buckled so that she clutched at the door for support.

She had run far and fast from the tall man who stood before her. She drew a trembling breath, torn between a logic that told her to slam the door shut and a growing elation at once again seeing Jason Bradley.

CHAPTER 4

JASON WAS MORE HANDSOME than she remembered.
His lean body carried the look of a natural outdoors-
man, rather than the carefully cultivated athletic build
of a man—like Lester—who spent the necessary
hours at the gym. His rugged appearance contrasted
sharply with a single soft pink rose that he held out to
her.

"We spilled the other one," he said tentatively. It
was a question, a plea for a new start.

Karaleen's mind raced back to the dinner on the
waterfront in Agricity. It skimmed over the scene with
the upset vase and the argument about the bill. It
fastened on the moments after when, beneath the
moonlight, Jason held her close.

"I would have been here sooner," he said, "except
it took all week to grow this thing." A sparkle in his
eyes belied his serious tone. "Besides, you don't
know how many other roses I needed for bribes,
trying to track you down."

Karaleen melted. How could she shut the door on
this disarming person? What harm was there in being

polite to someone who must have gone to a great deal of trouble to find her?

"I don't know how you got here, but," she smiled and half shrugged. "Hello, anyway." She reached for the rose in its slender, white vase. "Thank you. It's beautiful."

She studied the contours of the delicate pink petals, knowing that at the same time Jason studied her. She was glad she wore the velvet dress instead of the jeans that she might have put on to spend the day working in a hotel room. What should she do now?

She brushed at her bangs self-consciously. "Would you like to come in?"

Jason appeared ill at ease. "Is it all right?"

Touched, Karaleen surmised that Jason Bradley had never before entered a lone woman's hotel room. In fact she felt certain that he never did anything that might be considered improper.

She remembered the overflowing tray delivered shortly before by room service. "Have you had breakfast?" she asked.

"Sure."

Of course. He would have eaten at daybreak. "But that was probably hours ago, wasn't it?"

"Afraid so."

"Come on in. It so happens that I have a brunch for two ready and waiting."

Karaleen bustled about on the balcony, setting the dishes on the wrought iron table. She placed the silver and folded the damask napkins just so, feeling quite domestic and extremely happy that room service had been careless in filling her order.

"I hope you like fried chicken livers. If you don't, you can have all the sweet-and-sour wings."

Jason stood inside the room, a frown on his face.

"It's all right," she said. "You don't have to eat either. We have fruit compote and muffins. Look, some are blueberry. And here's two little waffles with strawberries and sour cream." He was still frowning. "Maybe you don't like any of this?"

"Oh, it all looks good," he assured her. "It's not that. It's just, well, you must have been expecting someone. I don't want to interfere."

Karaleen broke in, "No, I wasn't. Room service sent up a double order by mistake. I guess they thought because last. . ." she stopped, "somebody got his wires crossed."

Now why didn't she want to talk about Lester eating there the night before? It wasn't Jason's concern whom she ate with, or who was in her hotel room.

She carefully put the white vase with its fresh pink rose in the center of the little table and stood back, satisfied. "Won't you sit down?" she invited courteously, a child playing hostess.

Jason seated her and then positioned himself, taking care not to bump the table's wrought iron legs. He clasped his hands in his lap and waited.

It occurred to Karaleen that Jason might be waiting for more than the sake of politeness. Perhaps he was in the habit of saying grace before meals. She used to be. Had he done the same thing at the waterfront restaurant? She, too, clasped her hands and bowed her head. After a moment's silence, she looked up and waited. Jason followed her lead, and then they began to eat.

Karaleen's appetite deserted her, and she floundered for small talk, but Jason ate heartily. Finally, she asked, "What brings you to South County?"

"I was looking for a runaway girl."

"Of course you were," she mocked, "and I thought farmers were supposed to be an honest sort of people."

"It's true. She ducked out on me at a convention in Agricity. Haven't slept a wink since."

"You'll have to come up with a better story than that," she warned.

Jason sighed elaborately. "Well, think what you will."

"Seriously, isn't your AA-Bee Citrus somewhere up in the Central Valley? Oh, I know. You've come down to see a big league ball game."

"I told you why I'm here," Jason insisted.

Karaleen's coffee cup clattered in the saucer. She pushed back her chair and stood. "Come on now. Your boss sent you to pick up a tractor or something, didn't he?"

Jason laughed. "Well, I did bring the truck. But, my pickup wasn't exactly built to haul tractors."

"Okay, a load of fertilizer?"

"What if he did? We'll hollow out a nice soft spot for you to ride in," Jason promised. "It might be a smoother ride than in the front seat, and certainly a more fragrant one."

Hands on her hips, Karaleen demanded, "Hey, Mr. AA-Bee Citrus, what makes you think I'm going to ride anyplace with you, especially in a bed of fertilizer?"

Jason rose from the table abruptly, reaching just in time to steady the toppling white vase. "Heh-heh-heh!" he teased, throwing an arm across his face in imitation of an old-time melodrama villain. "Because, Ms. Vali-Turf, you wouldn't dare refuse a potential client."

Secretly Karaleen wondered how likely a customer Jason really was. "Help!" she cried, leaning over the balcony railing and waving both arms. "I'm trapped. Won't somebody rescue me from this fearful man who wants to steal me away hidden in a truckload of fertilizer?"

Jason dodged the table and rushed to Karaleen, crying, "Never fear, Jason Bradley's here." He pulled her to him, and swung her lightly into his arms.

Taken by surprise, Karaleen struggled to keep up the charade. She squealed, "Put me down, sir! You're supposed to be the villain."

Jason's face was close, too close, and with it came a provocative scent of after-shave. His arms held her tightly. For an instant, their eyes met.

Then swiftly he carried her inside. "In that case, here, take that."

And with a little toss, he dropped her on the bed. She bounced up from the quilted spread, laughing to cover her emotions. She brushed by Jason out to the balcony and furiously began stacking the dishes. She carried the white vase to the dressing room for fresh water. The mirror there revealed a flushed face, bright eyes. How could this man disturb her so? It was the kind of simple game any high school couple might have played. Yet through it ran a current far deeper than a simple game.

She stole a look at Jason. He seemed engrossed in the blank screen of the computer terminal until he turned and said almost formally, "I was hoping you would spend some time with me. I don't leave for home until tonight. I'll bring you back to the hotel whenever you say, if you have plans for this evening."

In the dressing room changing from the velvet dress into a pants outfit, Karaleen dismissed the excitement Jason generated within her. *Tomorrow, he'll be back on his farm. And soon I'll be back where I belong.*

"I'm ready," she called.

Whatever business Jason's boss had sent him on must not have involved hauling fertilizer after all. The truckbed was empty. She was surprised at Jason's ability to maneuver South County's freeway system. For a country boy, he seemed at home in traffic.

He confided to her that, because he lived some distance from the ocean, visiting the beach would be a treat for him. They took off their shoes and walked side by side.

Jason said little about himself. She gathered that on his job he was responsible for many acres of oranges.

He was thirty-two. He had never married because, "God hasn't seen fit to provide me with the right girl."

Feeling obligated to reciprocate, she offered, "I have to get my career established before I seriously consider marriage."

"Then what?" he asked.

She stammered. "Well, when the right fellow comes along, I'll . . . why, I'll get married. Lots of women have both career and marriage, you know."

"It's important to you, isn't it?" he asked. "Having your career, I mean? I suppose this computer stuff can get pretty exciting."

They had paused, and both stared out past the whitecaps. Strangely, the answer she gave seemed crucial. "Yes," she said slowly. "My career is important to me."

Jason picked up a small shell. With a heave, he hurled it over the water.

"But," she said almost to herself, "love is important, too."

Jason smiled at her, a gleaming, white smile that warmed her all the way down to her bare toes. As they walked on, she tried to shake the nagging feeling that he might have read something more into that statement than she had intended. She must be careful to limit the remainder of their time together to one of companionship. It wouldn't do to put serious ideas into Jason's head. The ideas whirling around in her own head were dangerous enough.

They walked near an excursion boat dock, and Jason suggested they take a harbor cruise. The tour guide was skilled at his recitation of famous persons owning the lavish homes that surrounded the harbor. Jason whistled as the guide related the typical cost per square foot of beachfront property.

After the cruise they came upon a roller skate rental booth. Watching skaters glide along the boardwalk between the sandy beach and the shops, Jason asked, "Want to try it? I warn you, though," he said, "I'm not too good on skates. Not many sidewalks where I grew up."

Karaleen vetoed the idea, not because of Jason's skating ability, but because he had already spent money on the harbor cruise.

Window shopping, they came to a street with several art galleries. Jason spied a watercolor of a sailing ship.

"My dad would like that one," he said emphatically.

Karaleen cautioned, "That probably costs a pretty penny."

But Jason insisted on going into the shop. Karaleen busied herself inspecting a collection of seascapes until Jason, wearing a disappointed look, turned away from the shop owner. "It's sold."

"Too bad," she said, relieved that he was saved the embarrassment of not having enough money.

As the sun set, Karaleen reminded Jason, "You said you had to leave tonight. Shouldn't you take me back, so you can start home?"

"Unfortunately, you're right."

"How long a drive is it?"

"Takes about four hours."

"Oh, you'll be so tired." How inconsiderate of his boss to send him all this way and not let him stay overnight before returning, especially on a Saturday night.

"Don't worry, it was worth it."

At the hotel, Karaleen said, "Please don't come up. You have such a long drive ahead of you."

But he insisted. After unlocking her door, he returned her key. She dropped it into her shoulder bag and then extended her hand. "Thanks for a lovely day." To disguise her edgy feelings she instructed, "If you get sleepy on the road, be sure and stop and run three and a half laps around the truck."

He chuckled, "Sure thing." He grabbed both her hands and squeezed so hard that they hurt, and then he was gone.

Karaleen told herself, "There! Nice day. Nice man. No harm done. I'll probably never see Jason Bradley again."

But later, alone on the bed and staring at the ceiling, Karaleen knew that the past hours had been among the most pleasant, the sweetest, she could remember. Resolutely, she got up and turned on the television. Nearby was the vase with the pink rose. She carried it out to the balcony, set it firmly on the table, and returned, closing the drapes behind her.

On Sunday Karaleen stayed in the hotel and threw herself into her work, both out of necessity to meet Monday's deadline for the auto parts program revision and because she felt a need to restore her usual intense interest in her work. As the day progressed her old satisfaction in a job well done returned. But the memory of Jason Bradley refused to disappear entirely.

Perhaps it was this renewal of enthusiasm for her programming work, rather than a desire to purge herself of interfering memories, but Karaleen entered the South County branch office Monday morning as a whirlwind of energy. She zipped through the final touches on the auto parts revision and took it to Lester.

"I knew you could do it. Piece of cake, wasn't it?" A sunburn from the weekend boat trip did little to detract from Lester's near-perfect image.

"Easier than that," she said with an air of confidence she hadn't felt since coming south. "What's next?"

"You sound as if a weekend away from me was just what you needed," Lester shot her a wary look. "I'm not sure I like that," he said. "But since you asked . . ." He opened a manila folder.

Karaleen felt ready to tackle anything. "Give me your poor, your hungry, your tired . . . your . . . give me everything," she offered generously. "I'll get it cleaned up and be on my way home."

"Slow down," Lester admonished. "Who said anything about your leaving? We've got a backlog here that's threatening to *break* our backs."

Karaleen suddenly saw tiny flashing red lights. "This is a temporary assignment, remember?"

"Of course it is," Lester said quickly. "It's just that, well, I don't know how we're going to get along without you."

Flattered, but still seeing the warning lights, Karaleen answered, "Vali-Turf's whiz kid will do fine with or without me."

Lester paused leafing through the papers in the manila folder. He looked Karaleen full in the face.

"Without you?" His eyes held hers. "That could get lonely."

She squirmed. He was getting too personal.

The next days passed quickly. Karaleen turned out volumes of work, despite minor irritations at the office. A template she had requested disappeared from the stationery store's delivery. It was found much later where it had mysteriously slipped behind reams of copy machine paper, after Karaleen had reordered. Thelma let her know that South County was not in the habit of ordering excess office supplies.

Karaleen noticed that she was the last person to receive mail, even though the receptionist passed her door at the beginning of her mail route. Once Karaleen stopped her and asked, "Anything for me?" The girl turned red, her eyes darting toward Thelma's office. She sorted through the envelopes, and with a weak smile handed Karaleen her mail.

Puzzled, but refusing to believe any sort of conspiracy, Karaleen responded, "Hope I didn't upset your routine."

Karaleen met Rosalie for lunch again. Rosalie invited her to the Tuesday night Bible study, but Lester had already asked her to have dinner with him and a client. Karaleen was secretly relieved, but she did make plans to go to Rosalie's church on Sunday. "That is," Karaleen hedged, "if I don't have to work."

She was struck again by the subtle changes in her friend. Rosalie seemed to possess an inner calmness that Karaleen did not remember from their college days.

Lester grew more and more attentive. They dined together each evening. Karaleen realized how closely their lives and their careers paralleled. Most of the time he kept matters on a professional level during office hours, and even after that, he never overstepped a certain familiarity. Still he managed to convey the definite impression that he was interested in Karaleen as a person rather than merely a fellow employee.

Karaleen found herself gratified and even flattered. She began to imagine what life with Lester would be like. She would continue working. It was possible that Lester would someday move on from Vali-Turf, but with their similar job interests, coordinating their positions would not present an unsurmountable problem.

On Thursday night they worked late in Karaleen's hotel room. Lester leaned back in his chair, his attention supposedly focused on the remote terminal's screen. Karaleen strolled out on the balcony for some fresh air.

She marveled at the twinkling lights below and the stars above. "I'm going to miss these lovely spring nights when I go back north," she mused almost to herself.

Her shoulders ached from hunching over the close work. She rotated them slowly in circles, trying to ease the cramped muscles. She raised her hands, reaching toward the starlit sky. She breathed deeply, closed her eyes, and stretched deliciously.

Suddenly Lester was behind her. His arms came hard around her waist. He whirled her to face him, and her own arms reached to his shoulders. Before she knew it his lips were on hers. It was a pleasing kiss, not wild, but decisive, deliberate. So like Lester.

"Don't talk about leaving." His voice was husky, and his hands were firm on her back.

She was shaken by this change from co-worker to suitor and struggled for a reply. His face moved close again. She disentangled herself, darting swiftly inside. "Goodness, Lester," she said, "you do take your employees to heart, don't you?" It was silly, but it was the best she could do.

Lester, now composed, seated himself at the terminal once more. "Yes," he said, with a knowing look in her direction, "and don't you forget it."

After he left that night it wasn't Lester's kiss that kept Karaleen awake. Nor was it yet another late telephone call that clicked dead when Lester answered. It was the memory of a moonlight walk by a black, glistening river with another man, a man who did not kiss her.

Friday morning Karaleen wanted badly to stay in the big, comfortable bed. Working so many hours each day was finally taking its toll.

At the office she placed her briefcase beneath the table in the cubbyhole she called home. This morning, a feeling of oppressiveness permeated the tiny cubicle. There was no room to put anything, even to breathe, it seemed.

The receptionist brought Karaleen's mail. Stepping over a telephone cord to reach the "in" basket, the girl tripped and lost her balance. She caught herself, but not before the heel of her shoe came down sharply on Karaleen's briefcase.

"I'm so sorry," the receptionist exclaimed. "Oh, no! Did I put that scratch on your beautiful brief-case?"

Karaleen tried to control herself. It wasn't the girl's fault. A contortionist would have difficulty maneuvering in such impossible quarters. "Don't worry about it," Karaleen said, trying to smooth out the scratch with her finger. But it was unlikely that anything would mend the gash cut into the beautiful leather.

Sadly Karaleen put the briefcase back under the table. But fury began to replace sadness. Her contact with Thelma had consisted of little more than a few "good mornings," which were grudgingly returned. Thelma certainly didn't initiate any friendliness. She always seemed busy. When not at her desk, she flitted about like a nervous chicken. What these continuous life-or-death missions were, Karaleen couldn't guess, but the girls under Thelma's supervision were kept constantly on their toes.

Karaleen had decided not to push for the office she knew she should have, hoping that, since it was Thelma's responsibility, she was making the arrangements. Karaleen was a professional employee, and as such, had always been treated courteously without having to make demands.

But today, with the gouged briefcase as a catalyst, Karaleen decided there was no choice. It was time to stop being pushed around. In order to regain respect in her own eyes and, perhaps in the eyes of other employees, she would have to take care of it herself, without going through Lester.

Karaleen tapped firmly at Thelma's open door. As she waited for acknowledgment, she thought that Thelma really was a rather attractive woman. She certainly dressed well and she wore the biggest diamonds Karaleen had ever seen. Definitely deficient in manners, Karaleen noted, waiting a full minute before Thelma lifted her head from a ledger.

"Yes?"

"Hello, Thelma," Karaleen forced cheerfulness. "Had your coffee yet? The girls out front were sweet enough to give me these." She offered a napkin on which rested two homemade cookies.

"No, thank you," came the quick answer. "I'll get some later, if I have time."

Feeling foolish, Karaleen tried to wrap the napkin around the cookies. She decided to act before she was rushed out. "About my office . . ."

Thelma waited.

The woman wasn't going to make it easy. Karaleen started over. "About my office, can you tell me when it will be ready?"

Thelma's cold gray eyes held Karaleen's without a flicker. "You must understand," she said crisply, "here at this branch, we are extremely busy. We seldom have time for anything except the most important tasks."

Karaleen wondered if she should laugh. Surely Thelma wasn't serious. Such abrupt rejection had to be her idea of humor, weird as it might be.

But Thelma continued, "It's not uncommon for an outsider to come aboard and, considering his—or her—work to be crucial, ask for special favors."

Karaleen's heart thumped wildly. Involuntarily she drew back. "I'm not asking for a special favor."

Thelma answered with a silent accusing stare and then turned her attention back to the ledger as if the matter were closed.

Karaleen gaped, feeling as insignificant as the moist crumbled cookies she clenched in her fist. *I can't let her get away with this,* she told herself. *Keep calm. Don't let her bully you. Just be reasonable. This has to be a misunderstanding. Clear it up.*

Aloud she said, "Surely, providing suitable working conditions falls under the heading of important tasks."

"At this office," Thelma assumed the role of patient supervisor, "we consider the actual work more important than the working conditions. Most of us are willing to sacrifice in order to get the job done."

All Karaleen knew about negotiating deserted her. Fury closed in. Thelma was not her supervisor. She searched frantically for a new maneuver in this incredulous battle. Finding none, she resorted to an out-and-out threat, "I am well within my rights to insist on an office suitable for my work and for my title." She scarcely believed that those words had come from her mouth. But she plunged on, bringing in the big guns. "And I believe there are," she paused for emphasis, "*others* who will agree with me."

Thelma did not flinch. "We always prioritize our tasks."

Just then Thelma's telephone mercifully ended the dreadful scene. Karaleen tried half-heartedly to smooth things with a final, "And I'm sure that an up-to-date organization like this gives proper weight to space environment."

Back in the little room, Karaleen grew more and more angry—angry with herself and angry at the situation she had been forced into. She packed her briefcase and left a message for Lester, "I'll be working at my hotel."

As she walked out of the office, she heard the receptionist caution an engineer on his way to Lester's office. "Thelma's in there." The girl grimaced.

Karaleen worked in her hotel room until after six o'clock, past the time when Lester would have called. She knew he was catching a plane at four, to be gone all weekend. She spent a rather lonely evening thinking how nice it would be to have Lester with her, and then caught herself wondering if she were focusing on Lester to avoid thinking of either Thelma or of the farmer in Central Valley.

She dutifully continued working Saturday morning, but decided to take the afternoon off. She called Rosalie, and they went shopping at the big mall that had intrigued Karaleen since her arrival in South County.

The mall was exciting. Karaleen had never seen anything to equal its shops, shops that were rather expensive, but with such varied inventories that she imagined one could find almost anything under the sprawling cover. Waterfalls and an arched bridge were only part of the pleasant atmosphere. She almost wished for her camera so that she could take a souvenir photograph as several tourists were doing.

Afterwards Rosalie invited Karaleen to her apartment, but Karaleen declined, saying, "It's Saturday night. Don't tell me you weren't planning on spending the evening with Rick."

"He won't be over until late. Come home with me."

For some reason Karaleen was reluctant to go back to the hotel room. Normally she would have enjoyed an evening with a good book. But, tonight, she succumbed to Rosalie's gentle urging and went to her apartment.

They chatted over iced tea. Karaleen had forgotten how easy it was to talk with Rosalie. They soon fell into their old relaxed manner and Karaleen found herself opening up about Thelma's mystifying behavior.

"I don't understand it, Rosalie. I've never had trouble being friends with anyone. I can't think of one other person that plainly dislikes me. As far as I know, I didn't do anything to offend her.

"One obvious question," said Rosalie, "are you endangering her job?"

"Goodness, no. I have no desire to be a threat to her, and couldn't even if I wanted to. She's firmly entrenched. From what I can tell, although she rules with an iron fist, she does a good job . . . except when I enter the picture."

"Sometimes people like that have hurts that we don't understand."

"Well, they should keep their problems to themselves," Karaleen grumbled and then softened. "Rosalie, you're so compassionate. I wish a little of that would rub off on me."

Rosalie laughed. "Compassionate? Remember some of the tricks we played on the underclassmen?" They launched into a giggling reminiscence.

Finally Rosalie said, "Maybe this thing with Thelma will work out. I'll pray about it."

Karaleen didn't know how to answer that, so she changed the subject. "Have you set a date for the wedding?"

They discussed Rosalie and Rick's marriage plans. Then Rosalie asked, "How are you doing in that department?"

Karaleen said, "So-so."

"Tell me."

"Not much to tell." But she did confide in Rosalie a little about Lester. "Our lifestyles are certainly compatible," she said.

"How exciting!" Rosalie commented dryly, and made a face. They both laughed.

"I'm afraid I put it badly," Karaleen admitted. "Really, it's more than that. And I think he wants it to be a lot more."

"What happened to that farmer you mentioned? The one you saw last week? I thought maybe . . ."

Karaleen glossed over her experience with Jason, trying to refute any false impression she might have given that there was anything between them. She summarized, "I don't see how he could ever be the one for me."

Rosalie sloshed the last bit of tea around in her glass. She studied Karaleen. "For some reason, I'm wondering if you really believe that. Is he a Christian?"

Taken aback, Karaleen thought a moment. "I guess," she said softly. "He hasn't mentioned church, but he did seem to want to say grace before we ate." Jason and Rosalie were a little alike, Karaleen realized, in some obscure, indefinable way.

"Are you, Karaleen?"

"What?"

"Are you a Christian?"

Karaleen mulled the penetrating question. "I'm not quite sure what your definition of a Christian is." Before Rosalie could respond, Karaleen posed a question of her own. "You've changed, haven't you Rosalie? I thought you were the same girl I knew, older and more mature, of course. But, it's even more than that, isn't it?"

Rosalie agreed, "I've changed. A while back, I became a Christian." She smiled at Karaleen's look of surprise. "Yes, I know, we always believed in God and called ourselves Christians. But, now, I'm a real Christian. I decided to accept Jesus Christ as what the Bible says He is—the divine Son of God and the only way to salvation. Ever since, well, I'm more at peace with myself than before."

Just then came a knock at the door. Karaleen stayed only long enough to meet Rick and to decide that Rosalie had indeed found herself a fine person.

The next morning she joined Rosalie and Rick at their church. It wasn't at all what Karaleen expected in light of Rosalie's new serious attitude toward religion. She expected a stilted service with a Bible-thumping minister preaching to an older congregation. Instead a great many of the two thousand people worshiping in the warm, beautiful sanctuary, were younger than she. And the sermon was Bible-teaching, not Bible-thumping.

Monday morning Lester stopped Karaleen as she

came to work. He led her into his office. "Got a surprise for you."

He opened the door to the room adjoining his. What formerly was a junkroom, now represented the epitome of a neat, efficient, fully furnished office. Even the terminal's cursor glowed, ready for use.

"It's all yours," Lester said proudly.

"Oh, Lester! It's perfect," she exclaimed.

She worked all week with a lighter heart than at any time since coming south. She tried not to think of the confrontation with Thelma. She was sure that Thelma had taken it to Lester. Karaleen was grateful that Lester had evidently backed her in the dispute.

Thelma treated Karaleen with a polite coolness, not much different than in the past. Karaleen hoped that Rosalie was right, that maybe things had worked out.

Lester continued seeing Karaleen most evenings. On occasion he would poke his head into her office during the day and, in a whisper, recall some shared moment from the evening before. Not that their evenings together held much that couldn't have been shared with the world, although Lester had taken to kissing her goodnight—never ardently, but quite purposefully. From time to time, he alluded to a future personal partnership.

Karaleen found herself becoming more and more comfortable with that idea. Lester was smart, ambitious, and stimulating. And she was attracted to him physically. She could do a lot worse than to marry Lester, she told herself.

The work was coming along well. She was anxious to report to Harry, but he was on a trip to the East Coast until Monday.

Saturday, she received a short letter from Jason: "I'm sorry I haven't been able to get down to see you again. I was hoping to get away this Saturday, but now it looks as if I'll be tied up. Be there as soon as I can."

Karaleen's damp fingers made soft prints in the paper as she read and reread the note. Jason had not come on business that day. She was sure of that now. He had driven four hours down and four hours back, just to see her. It was like he had said. He really had been searching for a "runaway girl."

She would have to put a stop to this. She ripped the note into the tiniest possible shreds. Jason Bradley did not fit into her plans. She must put him out of her life and out of her thoughts once and for all.

Lester, sitting at the terminal in her room that evening, proposed marriage. Karaleen accepted.

CHAPTER 5

THE ALARM ON KARALEEN'S pocket-sized calculator sounded early the next morning. She groaned and remembered it was Sunday and she had promised to meet Rosalie and Rick at church for the early service.

Karaleen sat through the unpretentious service with its straightforward message, a Bible borrowed from the hotel room on her lap.

Afterward Rosalie asked Karaleen to the apartment for brunch with her and Rick. Karaleen declined, and instead drove down to the beach.

The day was bright and clear, but cool enough to ward off many beachgoers. Karaleen walked miles along the uncrowded shore, pondering, among other things, why she had not told Rosalie and Rick of her engagement to Lester. She must call her parents in St. Louis, too. She would, but not until Lester was with her so she could introduce them over the telephone. And that wouldn't be until the next night. Lester was presently out with a client. He thought nothing of working on Sundays.

A couple approached Karaleen, their arms entwined. With eyes only for each other, they would have collided with Karaleen had she not dodged them. Today, it seemed that everyone on the beach had a partner except her. Lester would have to ease his work load a little after they were married, she decided.

On Monday morning Karaleen arrived at the office before Lester. She caught herself stealing glances toward the closed door that separated their offices. The feeling of anticipation of Lester's imminent arrival was new and exciting. She allowed herself the luxury of staring out the window deep in dreams, imagining what it would be like to be Mrs. Lester Peterson.

She heard a tap at the door and it opened to reveal the subject of her dreaming.

"Hi," she said, with an inflection she hoped conveyed the special welcome she felt. "I've been expecting you."

"Was held up with a phone call at home. Did you run the printout yet?"

Something like a cool breeze brushed over Karaleen. Of course she didn't expect Lester to rush in, sweep her into his arms, and cover her with passionate kisses. This was, after all, a place of business. *Still,* she thought wryly, *he had offered more in the way of a greeting before they were engaged, than a call from across the room asking for a printout.*

"No," she said, trying to conceal her disappointment. "I'll get right on it, though."

But Lester changed his mind. "It can wait. Come in my office so we can talk."

There, that sounded more like it. Karaleen did as he asked and waited expectantly while he shut the outer door. But Lester simply motioned her to a chair and took his own behind his desk.

"Darling," he began. She should be in his arms if he was going to talk that way. "I missed you yesterday."

"Me, too," she answered.

"I can hardly wait until . . ."

"Me, too."

She stretched her hands toward him. Realizing one still held a pencil, she dropped it on the smooth desktop.

He put both his hands over hers. "I wish we weren't here at the office." His grip was fierce.

Confident once again, she teased, "Afraid somebody will walk in on this scandalous scene?"

Lester's eyes darted toward the closed door. He pulled back, leaving her hands empty on the desk.

"Lester, I believe you actually are worried that someone will see you holding hands with me."

"Nonsense." The word crackled between them.

In the silence that followed, Karaleen told herself that Lester's tone didn't mean anything. It couldn't. At that moment, Lester himself sat across from her nearly perspiring with agony.

"It's just that—Karaleen, don't look at me like that. It's just that this is a professional office, and it might not look good for us to get personal during business hours."

"I guess not," Karaleen agreed.

"Some companies won't even allow a husband and wife to work in the same department," Lester reinforced his position.

"That makes sense."

"I knew you'd understand. I promise we'll tell everybody about us after we get a chance to make plans."

Karaleen began to comprehend what Lester was really saying. "You mean you want to postpone announcing our engagement?"

"It won't be for long, darling."

Karaleen's common sense told her that Lester was probably right. The disappointment she felt moments earlier was already fading, and in its place, was a whisper of . . . what? Relief? It couldn't be. Aloud, she agreed, "No, not for long."

Lester sat back in his chair, clasping his hands under his chin, index fingers tapping his lips in concentration. "We have your career to consider, too."

"Speaking of my career," Karaleen forced her thoughts to switch back to Vali-Turf business, "I'm going to put in a call to Harry and report on last week's work." Lester stiffened, almost as if in alarm. "Don't worry," she hastened to add, "I won't tell him about our engagement either."

"It's not that," he said quickly. "Ah, it's just that he's not in."

"Oh? I understood he'd be back today. Well," she shrugged and got up to leave, "I'd better get the printout done. The more I finish, the more I'll be able to astound Harry when I do call him."

"Karaleen," Lester said suddenly, "didn't you mention something about a friend of yours? Rosalie, isn't it? She wanted you to stay with her, didn't she?"

Puzzled, Karaleen nodded.

"You get along with her, don't you?"

Karaleen nodded again.

Lester moistened his lips. "I was thinking that it might not be a bad idea for you to move out of the hotel and stay with your friend for a while. Hotel rooms can get awfully lonesome."

Taken completely by surprise, Karaleen murmured, "Well, I don't know." She thought a minute. "Harry did send me to the hotel. It seemed silly to make more complicated arrangements since I was coming on a temporary assignment."

Lester gave her a piercing look. "Things have changed."

She caught her breath. "I guess I should think about it. I'll talk to—"

Before she finished, Lester had rushed over to her

and pulled her out of the chair. Briefly he crushed her against him, his mouth hard on hers. Then, just as quickly, he put her at arm's length, and said, "Love you."

Shaken but happy, Karaleen responded, "Is that what you call not getting personal?"

He pushed her out the door.

The rest of the day, Karaleen had difficulty keeping her thoughts away from Lester's rather odd manner. She tried to dismiss it, telling herself that becoming engaged could have the same unsettling effect on Lester as it did on her. As far as she knew, Lester had, up to this point, concentrated fully on developing his career, just as she had. Now, they each were faced with the dual channels for their time and energies. The change would take patience and understanding on both their parts.

In late afternoon, she received a call from Harry.

"I was going to call you," she told him, "except I heard you weren't back in the office today."

"I'm back now," he said needlessly. "What about?"

Karaleen mentally began to review the points she wanted to cover. "I don't have everything at my fingertips. You caught me by surprise. I wanted to go over last week's work."

"Is that all?"

Harry must be joking. "Is that all?" she said. "We're talking about a week's hard—and I mean hard—work. Don't you even want to hear about it?"

"Sure, sure," he said quickly. "Everything else okay?"

Harry was beginning to sound like he merely wanted reassurance that the building hadn't burned down. In fact she was reminded of her call to him when she had asked about selling her desk.

"Of course, it is. Now, that auto parts man—"

"Karaleen, you can tell me about him tomorrow."

"Oh?" *Harry must be in a hurry to get off the phone,* she thought. "What time shall I call you?"

"Don't call. I'll be there before noon."

"Here?"

"That's what I said. Didn't Lester tell you? See you then." And he hung up.

Karaleen checked Lester's office, but he was already gone. She drove to the hotel puzzling now, not only over Lester's unexpected behavior, but over Harry's call. A visit from Harry wasn't out of line. He kept close touch on his employees and his business. In fact, she was rather surprised that he hadn't been down before during the weeks she had been in South County. It was Harry's attitude on the phone that gave her an uneasy feeling.

Lester arrived at her door at seven to take her to dinner. For once, he wasn't accompanied by his briefcase.

Feeling the need of a lift, she had put on a new bright gold dress with a full, swirling skirt that she had found on her shopping trip with Rosalie. Lester showed his opinion of her appearance with an appreciative whistle. He took her in his arms and held her tenderly until she said they had better go before the dining room closed.

Lester's behavior seemed almost back to normal during dinner. He brushed off her question about Harry's visit with a wave of his hand, saying, "Oh, yes, did I forget to mention that?"

When he left he wheeled the remote terminal out with him. "Since you'll be moving, I might as well get this thing back to the office."

The next morning Karaleen heard Harry in Lester's office before he bustled into hers. He closed the door and paced around the room stopping to poke one finger into a potted fern as if to check the soil's moisture content. Catching sight of Karaleen's new briefcase, he uttered an admiring, "Wow."

When he finally took a chair, he began, "How's things?"

Karaleen eyed him suspiciously. Her relationship with Harry had always been good. She didn't like the idea of playing games with him, so she blurted out, "Fine. But what's really going on?"

As if he were dealing with a potential adversary, Harry countered in an unemotional tone, "That's what I came to ask you."

Karaleen didn't know what to think. She stammered, "I . . . I don't understand. Is something the matter? Did I ruin a job? Insult a customer?"

Harry leaned back and clasped his hands behind his head, continuing to study her. "I'm checking out a rumor."

Karaleen began to feel very uncomfortable. "A rumor? About me?"

"Partly."

Her mind raced back over the past weeks. What did she do that could possibly have interested Harry, let alone brought him all the way down here? She was at a loss. "You must know something I don't," she said. "How about enlightening me?"

"It's just a rumor," Harry said, "and, as far as I'm concerned it will never go beyond these walls. But, since it was brought to my attention, I have to investigate." Harry looked in danger of losing his cool demeanor. "It. . . ." He swallowed hard. Abruptly, he sat forward and demanded, "Darn it, Karaleen, are you behaving yourself? There's no hanky-panky going on between you and Lester, is there?"

"Hanky-panky!" she nearly yelled the words, after which she began to laugh, almost hysterically. "Oh, Harry, what an expression." But immediately she saw that Harry was not laughing. "No, Harry, I don't know what you heard, or who might . . ." She stopped suddenly, horrified at her own thought. She *did* know a likely candidate for starting a false rumor about her. It was hard to believe, but then, so was everything else about Thelma.

With a keen perception, Harry deduced her suspicions. "I think you know who might have called me. From what I understand, there has been a confrontation between the two of you."

Karaleen felt sick. Thelma had gone immediately for Lester's help in getting her way after Karaleen's first challenge—the business with the expense report. Now, Thelma had taken this method to punish Karaleen for her second challenge, that of insisting upon an office in which to work.

Karaleen tried to speak calmly. "Precisely what are the accusations?"

Harry's words hit like stones. "For openers, it seems that you have made unreasonable demands on the staff as far as office space is concerned and have refused to conform to the local office routines. In short, you're being difficult."

"This can't be happening. I hope you know me well enough to believe that I have bent over backwards to cooperate and not to cause trouble here. Do I have to drag out the dirty laundry and defend myself?"

Harry seemed somewhat satisfied. "Had to check it out," he said. But instead of relaxing, he coughed several times and said, "About the hanky-panky . . ."

"You're serious, aren't you?"

"When it comes to my employees fooling around, especially with Vali-Turf paying the bills, yes, I'm serious."

A knot of fear formed in the pit of Karaleen's stomach and began to grow. She tried unsuccessfully to will it away.

When Karaleen didn't respond, Harry continued, "I was told that Lester's been spending a lot of time in your hotel room." He paused significantly. "Until all hours of the night."

Karaleen knew he had already talked to Lester.

Why was he still questioning her? She must keep a level head. "We were working." This had gone beyond office protocol; she, as a person, was under attack. Above all, she must not cry. "Harry, we were working!"

Then, oddly, Harry did an abrupt turn-around. He reached over and patted her hand. "I just had to hear you say it." His eyes told her that was the truth, but still he added protectively, "Just be careful, okay?"

The sudden change did little to restore Karaleen's peace of mind because a phrase Harry had used in his grim questioning loomed before her like a dirty gray banner, "Until all hours of the night."

Karaleen jumped up, toppling a pencil holder, sending its contents flying. "That . . ." She floundered. ". . .woman! She must have made those strange telephone calls. Lester answered the phone, and each time it went dead."

She stormed across the room and was at the door before she caught herself. She slapped both hands over her face, breathing deeply. What a way for a professional career woman to act.

Ashamed, she returned and began gathering the spilled pencils. Her shaking fingers dropped more than she could replace in the holder. "Harry," she begged, her voice almost a whisper. "Get me out of here. I don't want to start acting like she does."

"Here," Harry said gruffly, "let me have that." He took the pencil holder and bent down, reaching under the desk for pencils, clearing his throat loudly. "Problem is," Harry, red-faced, got back in the chair, "Lester insists that you two make a great team, and that he really needs you a little longer."

Of course. Karaleen attempted to take a rational view of the situation. She should stay here, at least until she and Lester made their plans. Thank goodness Lester was thinking straight.

"He's promised to try and keep the office manager

off your back," Harry continued. "You know she does a great job for the company. Frees Lester from a lot of details. It's just that . . ."

"Yes," Karaleen said, woefully, "its just that she hates me."

Harry snorted, "Nobody hates you."

"Then you explain it."

Harry ignored that. "By the way, Lester is certainly pleased with your work. Brags about it as much as we do up north." He gave her a sideways glance. "Not to take away from your professional accomplishments, but could it be that he's interested in more than your work?"

Karaleen ached to confide in him that she and Lester were engaged. Instead, she said, "There you go, watching out for me again."

"Have to protect my investment in a valuable employee," he laughed. "My secretary tells me some fellow tried all week while I was back East to contact me about a job he wants you to do. You, and nobody else."

Later, on the way out of her office, Harry went fishing again, "One more thing I almost forgot to mention. It seems your hotel bill included brunch for two—in your room—on a Saturday. Lester couldn't explain that."

Karaleen could feel a blush in her cheeks and indignation at the suggestion she'd padded her expense account.

Harry winked, "A girlfriend, no doubt?"

"That was a mistake," she called, but Harry was striding down the hall.

Lester and Harry were busy the rest of the day. Karaleen didn't see Lester alone until that evening at the hotel.

By then she had resolved that her conversation with Harry was a thing of the past. She wouldn't hash it over with Lester, and was sure he wouldn't want to either. But she had to know one thing.

"Why didn't you tell me the reason Harry was coming?"

Lester put his arms around her. "You poor kid. Sorry you had to go through that. But honestly, I didn't know exactly why he was coming. I only had my suspicions. He drew her to him and ruffled her brown hair. "Say, how come you never told me that our boss has such a high opinion of you?"

"What am I supposed to do? Tell you about all the men in my life?"

"No," Lester said seriously, "I respect your privacy—up to a point, just as I know you respect mine. That's part of why our relationship will be a success."

Still, Karaleen wished Lester had confided in her about Harry's visit. But no doubt, he knew best. He certainly had taken precautions to combat any sort of rumor—keeping their engagement secret, initiating her move from the hotel. He had even taken the computer terminal back to the office. How like him to cover all the bases when it came to his career. *Their* careers, she corrected herself.

The next night Karaleen packed her bags and checked out of the hotel. Even though she wasn't as sure as Lester seemed to be that the move was important, she looked forward to a change from the hotel. The informality of apartment-living, especially so close to the beach, was appealing. How nice it would be to once again have a kitchen at her disposal. She left word at the hotel for mail and calls to be forwarded to the South County office.

Rosalie's apartment was cozy and attractive. But her warm greeting made Karaleen realize that more than anything she was happy to be with a friend. Wiping the tears, she sniffed, "This is almost like coming home."

Friday afternoon the receptionist buzzed Karaleen, "A Mr. Bradley is calling long distance."

A funny little spark of excitement surged through Karaleen, a spark she knew should not be there. She squelched it and, in her most businesslike manner, requested, "Please tell Mr. Bradley that I am in conference for the remainder of the day."

In an effort to avoid actual work with Thelma as long as possible, Karaleen lugged dozens of binders into her office where she dug out bits of information and pieced them together as best she could. This made the job twice as hard as it should have been. If only Thelma didn't dislike her so.

The first weekend at Rosalie's apartment Karaleen worked on Saturday, but informed Lester that she would drop if she didn't take Sunday off. She asked Lester to go with her to Rosalie's church but he said he should spend the day cultivating the customer who had the boat.

After church Karaleen drove to the beach. She walked and walked, gleaning relaxation in the feel of the soft sand under her toes, the fresh breeze tossing her hair. This time she had brought a sandwich and a beach towel. She stared out over the waves, never tiring of their loud, yet soothing roar. She mulled questions for which she could find no answers. She wondered how many other people in years past had sought answers to these same questions, perhaps in this very spot.

She found herself opening the paperback Bible—a purchase made during an impromptu stop at a Christian bookstore a few days before.

A small boy and a tall man passed between her and the water's edge. The toddler eagerly tugged ahead, trying to hurry the man along, until the little fingers slipped and the boy tumbled, falling into a patch of smooth wet stones left by the receding tide. Karaleen watched the man gently inspect the bruised knees. The boy's tears stopped and he squealed with pleasure as he was boosted up to the man's shoulders.

Jason would be like that, Karaleen thought, patient and caring with a child.

In a twinge of guilt, she told herself that Lester would be, too.

Karaleen had begun a new project at work. It was not one that she relished.

"But Lester," she protested, "anything to do with salesmen's reports sounds like the office manager's realm, and you know how well Thelma and I work together. Can't you assign someone else?"

"That's just it," Lester was firm. "This job has been on hold for a long time, waiting for an outsider, so to speak. You can be more objective than anyone else. We need something brand new—a system that computerizes and documents every aspect of our sales program, from the time spent in accomplishing each sale right up to sales projections for the entire branch. Don't worry, only a small portion has to do with Thelma, and she'll be glad to have you ease her work load."

In the days that followed, several calls came to the office for Karaleen from Jason. Each time she made an excuse not to take the call, ignoring the raised eyebrows of the receptionist.

Now when Karaleen and Lester worked after hours, it was at the office. They sometimes went to dinner and then back to the office. Or they worked straight through until eight or so. By then, both were too tired to care about dinner, so they often stopped at the pie shop. Usually after that they parted, and Karaleen would drive to the apartment.

She would look longingly at Rosalie and Rick spending their evenings together, sometimes engaged in a battle of wits over a parlor game, or often deep in discussion with their Bibles open in front of them. If friends were present, Rosalie would introduce her, and Karaleen felt nothing would make Rosalie happier than to discover a flicker of interest between Karaleen and one of Rick's friends. As she showered and fell into bed, Karaleen thought that, even if she had not been engaged, she would have been too tired to socialize.

Late one Thursday afternoon, Harry called her.

"You know that guy I mentioned that wanted you to do a job?"

"What guy?"

"Oh, I told you about him when I was there. Wants a whole business system. It might lead to more."

"I don't see how I can help him. I'm down here, and I've got my hands full."

"Lester is going to have to get along with you on a part-time basis for a while. I've already talked to him about it. This man insists you're the only one he'll deal with."

"You mean you want me to come back up north?"

"No need for that. One of his men will pick you up at the office tomorrow before noon. He'll take you to the site."

"But . . . but . . ." Karaleen cried, "who is it? What kind of job? Fill me in."

"Say, I've got a long distance call holding on another line. The guy's name is Arnold. The fellow who will pick you up is Chuck Creighton. You'll need to do payroll and everything else. You know, the whole bit. Check in with me next week."

"Wait, Harry. Be more specific."

"Oh, yes, throw a toothbrush in that fancy briefcase of yours. You'll have to stay overnight. You don't mind working on Saturday, do you?"

Without waiting for an answer, Harry said, "Do a good job for us," and hung up.

How like Harry to brush off details. Karaleen hurried to find Lester, but he was gone and had left word that he would be out of touch for the evening.

The next morning, the receptionist announced to Karaleen that her ride was waiting.

Lester was in conference. Karaleen hesitated at his door, her hand poised to knock. She decided against interrupting, however, and went on her way.

Her driver, a suntanned young man, seemed beset with a bad case of bashfulness. She confirmed that his name was Chuck Creighton and that he worked for someone named Arnold, but had determined little more when he stopped the rented car at the county airport.

"Plane's over this way, ma'am," Chuck announced.

Too embarrassed to admit that she hadn't been informed of any such travel plans, Karaleen meekly boarded the four passenger private aircraft.

She watched as Chuck readied the plane. "Are you the pilot?"

"Yes ma'am," he said politely, "I've had my license going on four years."

It was Karaleen's first time in a private plane. She sat in the front seat beside Chuck, careful not to move lest she break his concentration as he went through a checklist prior to takeoff. The radio issued sounds mostly unintelligible to Karaleen.

She held her breath as the plane left the runway and lifted over South County. She watched the metropolitan scene below become a diorama of miniatures. In the bright sunshine, swimming pools gleamed like flat blue lights. Streets unrolled in long bands of ribbon. Tiny specks scurried over a school playground.

Before Karaleen could become accustomed to the sensation of the small plane, and certainly before she had a chance to quiz the bashful Chuck regarding their destination, South County had slipped far behind them. Now gliding beneath the plane was flat land, marked off into neat plots—some smooth and green, some brown and waiting. Fields of tightly packed treetops began to appear. To one side rose a mountain range. The plane curved toward the mountains.

Chuck pointed out the window as they swooped down along a green area which appeared to be acres and acres of precisely planted trees.

They set down on an airstrip near a highway. Chuck took Karaleen's small suitcase to a station wagon. He was no more talkative on the ground than he had been in the air, but it seemed to Karaleen that he drove faster. Perhaps it was because of the evenly spaced, identical rows of trees whisking by the car windows.

After she asked, Chuck did say that it was a plum grove. Then he voluntarily identified a field of almonds, and some large spreading trees as walnuts. Scattered among the groves were open fields. Occasionally Karaleen glimpsed a house.

The scene changed. "Citrus," said her guide.

Even I can tell that much, Karaleen said to herself. "What kind?" she asked.

"Half navel. Half valencia."

They turned off the highway and followed another paved road. After several turns the car slowed although Karaleen could see nothing but more trees ahead. Without warning a paved drive appeared to the right of the road. The car turned between wooden gateposts so quickly that the letters carved into them blurred.

The drive circled in front of a large, rambling Spanish style stucco house tucked away in a mass of lush green citrus trees. The car stopped.

"We're here," announced Chuck.

Karaleen, still in a daze, asked, "Where?"

But the sight of a familiar figure striding across the freshly mowed lawn, provided the answer; along with a delightful, intense thrill that she quickly dismissed as merely surprise,

The car door opened. A strong, slightly rough hand reached to help her, and Karaleen stepped onto the grounds of the AA-Bee Citrus Ranch.

CHAPTER 6

JASON BRADLEY, HIS HAND still holding Karaleen's, wore the satisfied smile of a host welcoming his guest of honor at a successful surprise party.

They stood inches apart while the car moved on. "I—I'm supposed to do some work for a Mr. Arnold," Karaleen said weakly. She withdrew her hand and concentrated on the colored threads woven into the soft plaid of Jason's shirt. She must keep a reign on the rising excitement that enveloped her at being thrust into this strange situation.

She spied her briefcase resting nearby. Deftly stepping around Jason, Karaleen picked it up in a wordless announcement that she was ready to begin work.

A woman approached, smoothing her apron and adjusting her unruly salt-and-pepper curls.

"Ms. Hammonds," Jason said, "may I present Genevieve Franklin, the best cook in the Central Valley?"

A blush softened the woman's face as she mumbled an objection.

But Jason continued, "Genevieve keeps the house in order and also keeps all of us in line."

Genevieve lifted Karaleen's suitcase from the driveway and motioned to the briefcase, saying "May I take that for you?"

Karaleen's grip tightened on the briefcase. This was a business meeting. She wasn't going to forget it. "Thank you, but I'll need this."

Genevieve disappeared into the house, announcing over her shoulder, "Lunch pretty soon."

"When she says pretty soon, you'd better be waiting with your fork in hand," Jason said. "Perhaps you'd like to freshen up."

He led the way toward the house, past a well-groomed rose garden. The tan adobe structure with its red tiled roof was a perfect complement to the rich green background of the surrounding citrus trees.

Karaleen sighed with wide-eyed admiration. "It's everything a Spanish style home should be. Mr. Arnold must love it."

They crossed a wide veranda, and Jason opened the heavy double wooden doors. Karaleen stepped into a cool entry paved with cream colored tiles edged in a red scroll design that echoed the red in the tile roof. To the left was an open door, through which she saw a handsomely furnished office. To the right was a hallway that appeared to lead to a bedroom wing. Ahead, a black wrought iron railing rimmed the entry. The gleaming tile floor reflected the soft leaves of plants which looked almost too perfect to be real.

"Genevieve's also good with plants," Jason explained.

Beyond the decorative iron railing lay a spacious sunken living room with a huge stone fireplace. The furnishings mixed contemporary and antique, giving an appearance of elegant comfort. From the living room sliding doors opened to a brick patio. Karaleen could see the bedroom wing stretching along the right side of the patio, and on the left was a matching wing, which probably included more living and kitchen area, so that the brick patio was surrounded on three sides by the house.

In the center of the patio stood a high fountain of mosaic tile, its water glistening in the noonday sun. A lawn stretched beyond the patio and disappeared in a background of trees.

Jason ushered Karaleen down the hallway on the right, which did indeed pass a large master bedroom. At the end of the hall, they reached a pleasant green and white room. Snow white curtains hung at the windows, and a white and green quilted, calico print covered the double bed. Scatter rugs of brown, blended with light earth tones and touches of green, dotted the parquet floor and picked up the rich brown wood of the furniture.

"There's a bath through there," Jason motioned to an inner door on the far side of the bedroom. "As you can see, the sliding glass door leads to the patio."

As Karaleen started to thank him, she noticed that her suitcase had been placed on a luggage rack in the room. "There's my suitcase," she blurted out. Feeling foolish, she tried to explain, "I thought . . . that is, I assumed I'd be staying at a hotel."

"Don't you think you could be comfortable here?"

"Of course. That's not it." Karaleen was irritated that she felt so ill at ease. "After all, I'm here on business. I never expected to stay in a private home." She politely added, "Although it's certainly hospitable of Mr. Arnold."

It was Jason's turn to look ill at ease. Karaleen suddenly wondered whose idea these accommodations were—Jason's or his employer's.

As if reading her mind, Jason said, "You probably noticed that there are no hotels nearby, but we could drive you into town if that would suit you better."

"Oh, no, I'd love to stay in this beautiful house.

Who wouldn't? Why, it looks as if it's ready for the cover of a decorating magazine. But you're sure this has all been arranged?"

"Positive. As soon as you're ready, just slip out through the sliding door. We'll have lunch on the patio."

Karaleen unpacked her toilet articles and freshened her make up. She ran a comb through her hair. Even when she had finished, she rearranged her toilet articles, and then combed her hair again. She was beginning to feel nervous at the idea of sleeping in a house belonging to a man she had never met.

When she could delay no longer, she made her way through the sliding door. Jason was waiting. In a shaded portion of the patio a round table had been set with brown linen placemats and white napkins edged in brown piping. A white ceramic bowl filled with teal blue irises brightened the center of the table.

Jason held a chair for Karaleen. As he seated himself opposite her, she realized that the table held only two place settings.

Trying not to sound like a scared schoolgirl, Karaleen asked lightly, "It's just the two of us?"

Before Jason could answer, Genevieve appeared with bowls of chilled cucumber soup. Obviously there was to be just the two of them.

From across the patio, in the kitchen wing, came the sound of men, probably at lunch. Above the conversation could be heard Genevieve firmly ordering someone to go back and wash, "And go all the way to your elbows."

Jason winked at Karaleen and explained, "If anyone comes to Genevieve's table with field dust, he usually ends up eating out in the field."

"I think I like Genevieve's no-nonsense policies."

"You would appreciate them." But Jason smiled so engagingly that Karaleen had to smile back.

He excused himself once and went into the house.

Karaleen heard him talking to the men, who were evidently on their way back to work.

After lunch he seemed in no hurry to get on with their business. Karaleen felt perhaps he was taking a leisurely lunch because of her. She wouldn't want him to get into trouble on her account, so she decided to get underway, "My boss didn't give me much to go on. I'm completely in the dark about AA-Bee Citrus. Do you think you could give me some background, at least until Mr. Arnold gets here?"

Jason responded quickly, "I should be able to do that. What do you need to know?"

"For starters, how big is it, how many employees, your present bookkeeping methods. Mostly, I will need to know what you want the computer system to do for you."

"It was my understanding that Vali-Turf would outline the marvelous capabilities of all its systems, and I would simply choose what I want."

Defensively, Karaleen retorted, "You make it sound like shopping in a candy store. After I know exactly how your operation works and what you want to accomplish, I can offer you a system that will incorporate everything you think you want plus a lot more than you ever dreamed of."

As she spoke Karaleen caught a hint of a smile on Jason's face, which rapidly faded. Had he been teasing her? She remembered how knowledgeable he seemed at the computer show in Agricity.

Then another thought struck her which brought with it a wave of embarrassment, not just for herself, but also for Jason. Perhaps he didn't have the authority to go into all this. Perhaps he was merely playing the part of executive until Mr. Arnold took over.

She spoke kindly, "Maybe you'd like to show me how this place actually runs, that is, while we wait for Mr. Arnold."

"Good idea," he said, taking a last swallow of ice water. "We'll get to the paperwork later."

He stood and then looked gravely down at her. She realized he was staring at her legs.

She shifted her feet and peeked to see if she had run her stockings.

"Did you bring anything else to wear?" he added.

"Like what?"

"Ah, something less dressy?"

"You mean pants?"

"Great."

She wished she had thrown a pair of jeans in her bag, but the gray slacks and pale yellow blouse she had brought would have to do.

Jason was waiting for her in front of the house. He leaned against an open four-wheel drive jeep that looked as if it had put in a long tour of hard duty on the ranch. An assortment of tools and equipment was in the back and strapped to the sides, of which Karaleen recognized little more than a shovel and a picnic cooler and a bucket.

"You'll have to explain everything to this city kid," she told him, as they pulled out of the drive.

Jason braked abruptly. He indicated groves on both sides of the road. "Those are trees—citrus trees," he said seriously.

Karaleen laughed. "That's about the only thing I do know. Chuck told me they were, half valencia, half navel. I gather that means half of them are Valencia oranges and half are navel oranges, or," she teased, "have you invented some new kind of hybrid?"

"Working on that one." Jason eyed Karaleen with an expression that plainly showed a sense of pleasure in her company.

Karaleen brushed her dark hair back from her face. The bright sun warmed her, or was it merely a cozy feeling generated by the knowledge that someone wanted her near and made no secret of it?

They drove first the perimeters of the grove that surrounded the house.

"How do you know what's a navel, and what's a Valencia?" Karaleen asked. "The trees all look alike to me."

"This late in the spring, chances are that the trees you see with *orange* oranges are Valencias."

"Sounds terribly scientific."

"Oh, it is," he assured her, and then laughed, "Most of our navels have already been picked for the season."

They turned down a lightly graveled surface between two rows. Lush, dark green foliage rose fifteen or twenty feet above the ground, forming a corridor whose walls of prolific branches reached to meet Karaleen's exploring fingers.

Jason got out to inspect a small section of young trees. He dug his boot in a berm of freshly-graded dirt. "We had a drainage problem here. These trees are replacements for the trees we lost."

Karaleen strolled through the rows alone while Jason talked with two men who were repairing irrigation lines. Underfoot, the ground was a spongy carpet of mulch—shredded prunings, Jason had said. She caught a whiff of orange blossom perfume as she entered an area of the grove where white, fragrant flowers hung from the branches.

It was so peaceful, so complete. No wonder that Jason felt pride in his work. This grove resembled a carefully tended garden. She pressed her face to a cluster of white blossoms and drew a satisfied breath.

But the breath caught and twisted into a cry of dismay. Beneath the tree was a sight that made Karaleen cringe. She jumped back from the unpleasant mound so close she had nearly stepped on it. She whirled and ran down the row, trying to put out of her mind the sight of raw, wet flesh, mixed with naked bones, and dotted with ragged bits of fur, which lay crumbled on the ground.

Jason must have heard her cry. He came running through the trees.

She pulled up short and, seeing the alarm in his face, called out, "It's nothing."

Without breaking his stride, he reached her. "Something must have frightened you."

"It shouldn't have," she said contritely. "I told you I was a city girl. But here in this idyllic setting, to see dead . . . oh," she repressed an involuntary shudder. "It was some kind of animal, torn to pieces."

"We tend to forget about things like animal instincts." Jason sent her on down the row and went back to speak to one of the nearby men before catching up with her.

Karaleen was almost glad the incident had occurred. It served as a reminder of how foreign rural life could be for her.

Back on the paved road, Karaleen asked about the propellers stretching high above the treetops, resembling streamlined windmills.

"Wind machines," Jason said, "for frost protection." He turned into the trees again. "Here, we'll take a look."

They approached a large engine resting on a concrete platform at the base of a tower. Jason motioned to a fuel tank nearby. "This one is a diesel machine. Some are electric. They all cost a fortune to run, but it's the only way to save a crop some winters."

"What about the smudge pots I've seen in old movies?"

"Labor and fuel costs have made them a thing of the past, even without considering pollution."

"How can those slim propellers help?" Karaleen asked.

"When turned on, they stir up the air in the grove. This motion prevents the cold air from settling down between the trees, so the temperature around the trees stays a little higher than it would without the wind. Of course, with a mist irrigation system," he pointed down to a network of slim, flexible black pipe snaking between the trees, "when there's danger of frost we pump water through the system as if we were irrigating. That helps, but if that's not enough, we resort to the wind machines."

Back on the road, Karaleen felt a pang of guilt. This was more like a lark in the country than a business consultation. "Shouldn't we be going back now?"

"Let's take a ride first. You haven't seen the largest grove yet." He leaned toward her confidentially, "This one is all Valencia."

"More trees? AA-Bee seems to be quite an enterprise."

They crossed an irrigation canal the width of a river, with a current almost as swift. The land ascended gradually, reaching toward the foothills at the base of the mountain range. Ahead appeared to be the last vestige of agriculture carved out of the foothills. Cultivation ended at a line of boulders buried in the foothills by some giant earth movement eons ago and now standing guard against further encroachment into its hilly domain.

Jason stopped on the road, pointing to a grove of trees that were noticeably smaller than those lower on the valley floor. "This is a marginal area," he explained. "You can see that these are young Valencias, planted only after the best flat land was taken."

"Oh, Jason," Karaleen said with a whim, "could we pick oranges?"

"Well, the sugar content won't be. . ." Jason began and then laughed, "Sure we can."

Feeling like a child on an unexpected holiday, Karaleen ran from tree to tree, picking the biggest fruit she could find. She hugged the round oranges to her body, trying to gather just one more. Jason laughed as one rolled out of her arms, and she bent to retrieve it, only to lose two more. Finally, he brought a bucket and held it while she let the bright orange balls roll in.

Then he took out a white handkerchief and gently brushed at her arms. "The oranges get kind of dusty," he said, his voice more rough than his touch.

"Here," she reached for the handkerchief, "I can do it."

"Hold still," he ordered, carefully dabbing at the tip of her nose. "Close your eyes." He wiped her cheeks with elaborate care. "There," he inspected her gravely. "Hey, wait a minute." He started brushing at her hair, as if flicking off bits of debris.

"Oh, come on," she laughed, knowing he was teasing. "Race you!"

Jason grabbed up the bucket and still outran Karaleen. She tripped just when she neared him, and he steadied her as she climbed into her seat.

They left the grove, heading higher. Karaleen challenged him, "I may be a stranger, but something tells me this is not the way back to the ranch."

"It's the way to dinner."

"Up here?"

"Wait and see."

Jason rounded the end of the grove and took a narrow road through boulder-covered hills. Soon they emerged on a plateau. Jason parked and came around to stand by Karaleen. In front of them spread the Central Valley, fading into the distance. Behind rose the Sierra Nevada Mountains.

"It takes your breath away," Karaleen whispered. "I had no idea that farmland, just farmland," she struggled to express herself, "could be so beautiful."

Something drew her eyes from the compelling scene toward Jason. He was watching her intently.

"I hoped you'd like it," he said, as if her opinion were important.

Quickly Karaleen jumped to the ground and moved

a safe distance away. "Didn't I hear somebody mention dinner?"

"Coming up!"

To Karaleen's surprise, Jason grabbed the picnic cooler from the back seat and produced a blanket from somewhere. "Don't just stand there," he demanded, "bring some of those oranges."

Side by side they watched the sunset, the picnic cooler resting primly between them.

The evening grew cool. Jason drifted away and returned with two jackets. He dropped one over her shoulders.

When the sun vanished from sight, leaving only a few colorful rays streaming upward from the horizon to spray a last bit of color over the clouds, Jason said in a voice that neither accused nor reproved, "You didn't return my calls."

"I know."

"That's why I tricked you into coming." His was a flat statement of fact. "I was hoping . . ." Suddenly Jason's tone changed to one of pleading, as if it were vital that he know, "Karaleen, what do you want? What do you really want in life?"

Karaleen's stock answer leaped to her lips. Mechanically, without hesitation, she replied, "An interesting career, and—someday—marriage."

In the distance, clusters of lights, glowing through the twilight joined together and formed a city. Scattered wide over the landscape were other pinpoints of light—farmhouses—homes with warm, loving families.

A light breeze rustled the sparse grass around them.

She didn't mean to say it, but some inherent compulsion for honesty came to the forefront. "But, lately . . ." She caught herself.

"Yes?" Jason encouraged.

"Nothing," she said firmly. "Just meandering thoughts." She musn't go on like this. She rose. "I think it's time we started back. I am supposed to be working for Mr. Arnold, you know."

But Jason didn't move. "Karaleen, you're a Christian." His clear, sincere eyes sought hers.

Karaleen sank to her knees on the blanket. She shook off an uncomfortable deceptive feeling. She *was* a Christian, wasn't she?

He continued, "Where does God fit into your plans?"

No stock answer for that. She would have to ad lib. "He's in my life, helping me, I hope, to make the right decisions."

All at once, Karaleen wanted desperately to confide in Jason, to tell him how, of late, misgivings had pushed her toward a re-evaluation of her relationship with God. Suddenly, whether it was the fresh, open setting or the gentle probing of this sincere man Karaleen wasn't sure, but for the first time, she knew her suspicions were true. Something was wrong between her and God.

But she couldn't talk about it to Jason. She might tell him of other doubts she had. It wouldn't be loyal to Lester. Lester!

She bolted to her feet, nearly knocking over the picnic cooler. She snatched it and whisked it toward the car. Jason followed slowly.

On the way back to the farm, Karaleen talked incessantly of concepts she had begun to form concerning the computerizing of the ranch's business operation. "I'd like to start work tonight, if you think Mr. Arnold won't mind. My, I can't imagine what he will think about us being gone the whole day."

Then another thought struck her. She sobered, almost at a loss for words. "Jason," she murmured, "is he married? I mean, who is going to be there at the house tonight?" She felt her face grow hot and was thankful for the darkness to mask some of her embarrassment. She didn't want to totally destroy her image as the liberated career woman.

Jason broke his long silence, as if glad to be rid of his thoughts. "Oh, if you're worried about the proprieties, don't. You'll be the only person staying in the house. Arnold is away on a trip."

"You mean, I won't even meet him? How will I know what kind of a system he wants?"

"I think I can help you with that."

Once again, a nagging question surfaced. Did Jason have the authority to act for his employer in such an important matter? She thought farm managers just managed land and crops and supervised the employees.

Then a thought hit her so quickly that she blurted it out without thinking, "Where do you sleep, Jason?"

Immediately she was sorry. Before he could answer, she raced to make amends. "I'm sorry. That's none of my business."

Jason answered softly, "I have a little place near the house."

She knew she had hurt him. She ached with fury at herself. This man had never given the least indication that he would behave other than as a perfect gentleman.

They pulled into the circular drive. Jason indicated the bedroom wing of the house. "My place is out that direction. I'll show it to you tomorrow, if you like."

He walked her to the veranda, but stopped short at the doorway. "Help yourself to anything in the kitchen. You won't disturb Genevieve. Her quarters are separate from the house beyond the kitchen." Almost before Karaleen could offer a brief thanks, Jason turned on his heel and walked away.

Inside, the open door of Mr. Arnold's office reminded Karaleen that she had not even stepped over its threshold. As she showered and prepared for bed, she put down a feeling of guilt with plans for an early start the next morning. She slipped between the green and white printed sheets, thinking that this day had been a total loss as far as the job was concerned. But except for the few minutes of self-examination Jason had forced on her, this was also one of the most delightful days she could remember.

Sometime later, Karaleen roused. She had dropped off to sleep so easily, but now, she tossed restlessly. Doubts, guilt, and worry crowded out the sweet, contented feeling she had taken to bed with her. Miserable, she rose and wandered about the room. She thought of turning on a light and looking for something to read, but the brightness of the moonlight coming through the windows was so lovely that it seemed a shame to wash it away.

She tucked her feet into slippers and drew on a short robe of the same misty green as the gown she wore. Perhaps if she just walked a bit she would be able to go back to sleep. She rarely had trouble sleeping.

Karaleen eased the sliding door open and crossed the patio. She followed a path around the bedroom wing and back toward the side of the house. Here was a portion of the grounds where she had not yet been. The bright moon illuminated a lawn area. Instead of citrus, large overhanging walnut trees formed a majestic half-circle around the spacious side yard. The night air was cool. Karaleen drank in its freshness, knowing but not caring that she invited a bout with pneumonia by venturing outside in such attire.

The glint of moonlight on something beneath one of the spreading walnut trees drew her attention. From a thick limb hung an old-fashioned wooden swing, the kind so prevalent on front porches during her childhood.

Forgetting her chill in the pleasure of such a discovery, Karaleen went to the swing. Tentatively, she pushed herself back with one foot, stretched her legs out, and swung forward. Sentiment carried her into the past as she settled into a graceful, swinging motion, propelling herself with only a touch of one slipper against the earth beneath the swing. Her soft robe fluttered, and her brown hair bounced ever so gently against the back of her neck.

Suddenly something alerted her. Listening, she heard nothing more than the restful creaking of the old swing and the peaceful night sounds. Yet, someone was near. Curiously, she felt no fear, and when her eyes focused on a tall figure leaning against the gnarled trunk of a nearby tree, it was as if she already knew that Jason was there watching her.

The swing continued its easy glide.

Karaleen broke the silence. "I loved these swings when I was a child."

Jason said nothing, his face in the shadows, one hand jammed into the pockets of his jeans.

Karaleen fingered the smooth slats of the seat beside her. "It's a shame that houses don't have swings anymore."

She felt the tension pulling between them as surely as if he were reaching his arms to her.

In a voice so low, so filled with emotion that she barely recognized it, Jason said, "Some houses still do."

Karaleen knew then that the swing was hers for the taking. And, at that moment, she wanted Jason there beside her. She wanted to lay her head on his shoulder and let him rock the swing back and forth.

The night sounds had stopped. There was only the rhythm of the swing. Out of the shadow Jason took a single step, one hand holding the trunk of the tree, the other grasping at a limb above his head, as if to anchor himself.

Then with a muffled exclamation, he retreated and was gone.

Shivering violently, Karaleen jumped up and ran to the house. Behind her, she heard the swing's soft creak dying into a lonely sigh.

CHAPTER 7

THE NEXT MORNING KARALEEN'S eyes opened briefly to a room filled with bright sunshine. She closed them again and stretched luxuriously, enjoying the feel of the smooth sheets. She floated in a green and white dream world, tethered to reality only by the slender thread of some vague exciting memory.

The memory grew sharper until Karaleen realized at its core was Jason and their meeting under the walnut trees. She jumped from bed, and after a glance at the time, hurried to dress and begin the day.

In the kitchen Genevieve waved her hand indicating the general direction of the mountains and reported that Jason was tending to a problem with one of the pumps. Knowing that everyone else must have eaten hours before, Karaleen refused Genevieve's offer of a hearty breakfast and suggested instead that toast would be sufficient. Genevieve was insistent, and as a compromise Karaleen carried fruit with her toast and coffee to the patio.

After the second cup of coffee and convinced she had allowed herself far too much luxury, Karaleen decided she simply had to get started on Mr. Arnold's job. It was out of the question for her to poke around in the office alone since Jason hadn't so much as cracked a ledger for her, but she brought her briefcase to the patio and began to put on paper the ideas that she had formed the day before.

Karaleen was still at the table, immersed in her work, when Genevieve brought lunch.

Karaleen glanced at her watch. To her surprise, it was nearly one o'clock. "Genevieve, I'm supposed to leave at two!" Her sudden dismay at the thought of leaving without seeing Jason, Karaleen assured herself, was only because she needed information from him before she returned to South County. She asked, "Is Chuck here?"

"He stopped by earlier on his way to town to get a part for that pump motor." Genevieve shrugged and went back to the kitchen.

Just then Karaleen heard the sound of boots on the patio behind her. She bit her lip and forced herself to turn slowly.

Jason stood there, his jeans dusty, black grease smeared from his hands to the rolled shirt sleeves of his plaid shirt. His dark hair was damp and still bore the crease from the wide-brimmed straw hat he held in his hand.

Karaleen searched his face. Would he ignore their encounter of the previous night?

He grinned, displayed his dirty hands, and said, "Don't worry, I won't get too close."

She relaxed. He was once again the easy-going manager of AA-Bee Citrus. She must follow his lead. "At least one of us is earning his keep. I'm afraid Mr. Arnold may not be pleased with my output these two days."

"I'm sorry you had to wait."

From inside the house came the ring of the telephone. "It's long distance," called Genevieve.

Jason wiped his hands across his jeans and scraped his boots before entering the kitchen wing.

Minutes later he returned. "Your office is on the phone. You can take it on the extension in your room."

How like Jason to automatically think of privacy for his guest's phone call. Aloud, she speculated, "Harry probably thinks I'm finished here and has me booked to a job in Alaska."

"Actually," Jason corrected her, "it's a Lester Peterson."

Karaleen's fingers clutched the latch on the sliding screen door. "Lester?" she cried. Then stiffly, "What a surprise," to cover the stab of. . .what was it? Conscience?

"I mentioned to him that we hadn't quite finished here," Jason said casually. That was an understatement.

He went on, "I suggested that it might be well if you met some of the other growers, to get more of an overall picture of the citrus industry."

Karaleen's mouth opened in a wordless protest.

Jason continued, "Tonight at a meeting in town. There didn't seem to be any objection on his part."

"Tonight? I'm leaving in an hour."

"No problem. Chuck can fly down to South County tomorrow afternoon just as well as he can today."

"The idea is preposterous," Karaleen exploded. "I came here on a twenty-four hour business trip. Besides," she frowned suspiciously, "a growers' meeting on a Saturday night?"

Jason's boot traced the cracks between the patio bricks. "It *is* the growers' association," he admitted, with that same boyish pleasure he had shown the day before when he had greeted her in obvious satisfaction at having executed a coup, "but it's more of a dinner."

Karaleen took a deep breath. "No," she announced

111

firmly. "I should leave this afternoon. My plans are already made." She stopped short of asking why he thought he had the right to appropriate the remainder of her weekend. She shoved the screen door along its tracks.

Lester wouldn't like the idea of her staying away another day. He would want to spend at least a part of the weekend with her. She could be sure of that. Even during the busiest of times, he squeezed out a few hours for her, didn't he?

She turned back to Jason, "No, I really can't stay here. You can answer some questions and give me a peek at your bookkeeping system. I'll just have to contact Mr. Arnold by phone for whatever else I need."

Inside, Karaleen listened as Lester engaged in pleasantries while waiting for the click that told them the receiver in the kitchen had been replaced. Then, his tone changed, "I miss you, Karaleen. Nothing's the same without you." Then it changed once more, "The citrus man says there are still some loose ends to tie up."

"I can get the rest of what I need by telephone," Karaleen assured him. "I'll be home by late afternoon. How about going down to the beach tonight? We could get some of that yummy shrimp and—"

"You know," Lester hadn't seemed to hear her, "that suggestion of his about your meeting the growers isn't half bad. You might come up with some good ideas talking to them."

"Lester, this isn't that big a job." She didn't want to tell him it appeared to her that AA-Bee Citrus needed only a packaged farm program and the proper hardware to run it, and moreover, that Jason might not have the authority to order even that. "Don't look for too much in the way of a big system."

"Well, Harry is certainly expecting something big. I think we'd better not let this guy get away from us. You stay over, huh? Go and meet his friends."

112

"But what about—?"

"What's the matter?" Lester chuckled. "Don't have a thing to wear?"

"As a matter of fact, no. I think it's a dinner."

"Well, go somewhere and buy something. They must have stores up there."

"It's not that," she pleaded, "I don't like the idea of working all weekend. We need time together."

"I know, I know," Lester soothed. "We'll see each other every night next week, I promise. You'll get sick of my hanging around. Besides, I promised that guy with the new line of printers that I'd take a look at his stuff tomorrow. He's been pestering the dickens out of me."

Karaleen sank to the bed. "Lester," she implored, "I don't want to stay." She glanced through the window. Jason squatted on the bricks, idly petting a calico cat that rubbed against him. He was a paradox of gentleness and strength, peppered with a boyishness that surfaced when it came to arranging things his way. Unsettled as she was, she smiled at how he had engineered this escapade, turning a simple business trip into a weekend vacation for two. She watched his powerful hands on the furry kitten, until she could almost feel them on her shoulders as they had been that moonlit night by the river.

Lester was still talking. Karaleen interrupted, a note of desperation in her voice, "I can't stay here."

"It's only a few more hours. I'll see you early Monday morning. Bye, baby. Now you charm those growers. Make all the contacts you can, but remember, you're mine."

Karaleen stalled her return to the patio. She spent far more time than necessary smoothing the green and white calico spread. She tried to shake the feeling of hurt left by Lester's call. She told herself that the last thing Lester would want would be for her to stay at AA-Bee Citrus if he realized the irrational thoughts tumbling through her mind. But she couldn't tell him that this ranch manager was doing crazy things to her emotions. She couldn't let on that one unsettling question after another kept surfacing and that all her determination was required to snuff them out.

Moreover, Jason musn't suspect any of this. It was crazy, but she seemed to be experiencing some sort of girlish infatuation. Well, she would extinguish it as of that very minute. Her marriage and career plans had not changed one iota.

If only she could confide in Jason about her engagement. That would settle everything. Perhaps it would be all right to tell one person. This was, after all, a special circumstance. If Jason knew, well, that would squelch his romantic notions quickly, thoroughly, and forever more. Yes, telling Jason would be like closing a door . . . so final . . .

But hadn't she promised Lester that she wouldn't tell a soul? Of course, she had. It would not be right to go back on her word.

She marched out to the patio. From her briefcase, she pulled a clean yellow lined tablet. "Seems I'm still on duty," she said.

If Jason sensed her embarrassment at obviously being overruled, he gave no indication other than an apology, "I hope this doesn't inconvenience you."

"Of course not!" Her denial was too sharp. But better that he think that than to suspect the real turmoil he was causing. "I didn't have any plans for the weekend anyway," she tried to laugh.

Jason bounded to the table and snatched the yellow tablet from her. 'What you need is to forget about computers for a while and have some fun."

Karaleen studied the handsome man before her, marveling at the clarity of his eyes, his engaging expression. No, she had not changed her mind about her career, or about Lester. So there was no reason why she couldn't have a good time with Jason. Lester

114

had more than given his blessing. And it was surely her own fantasies that made her think Jason was interested in anything more than, as he suggested, having some fun while the boss was away.

"Take me to the most expensive shop in the nearest metropolis," she said gaily. "I don't want you to be ashamed of me in front of your friends tonight."

"Fat chance," Jason snorted.

To Karaleen's surprise, the small dress shop where Jason drove her boasted a good selection. Almost immediately she found the perfect dress, in shimmering forest green with a subtle overall tone-on-tone pattern. It was real silk, much too expensive for her personal pocketbook, but this dress was going on her expense account. A fleeting picture of an outraged Thelma checking the weekly report came to mind, and Karaleen patted the price tag kindly.

She was in such high spirits as she told the salesgirl to wrap up the dress that the girl remarked, "This must be for a very special occasion."

"Not really," Karaleen answered with a shrug, as if spending that kind of money was something she did every day of the year.

Jason gave her a tour of the town. It was actually a small city, complete with two enclosed shopping malls. On the way back to the ranch, he turned the station wagon off the highway and detoured through a little community. He pointed to an older white clapboard building. "That's where we'll go to church tomorrow."

That evening, Karaleen gazed into the mirror, checking once again the fit of the new dress. She was even more pleased with it now, but at the same time began to worry that she might be overdressed for the growers' dinner. She would ask Jason if she should change into the tailored suit she had traveled in.

The doorbell rang. Genevieve was visiting relatives, so Karaleen walked down the hall, across the tiled entry, and paused. Reeling under the heady effect of the expensive dress and the gracious setting, Karaleen swung the door wide. She was a princess welcoming her prince—her entire court having been dismissed in the interest of privacy.

In such a fanciful mood, it was no surprise to find Jason there, looking every bit the part of a prince, with a single pink rose in his hand. One glance at him and she knew her dress was right for the occasion. Jason wore a beautifully tailored dark suit that accented his slim figure. The boots were gone, and in their place were black dress shoes.

But his nearness abruptly shattered her illusory role of nobility. She clutched her white sweater, feeling like a teenager on a first date, while Jason found a vase for the rose. "My, I should have picked up a mink stole while we were in town," she quipped feebly.

Jason's eyes swept over her. "You look perfect just as you are, but hold on a minute."

He disappeared into the master bedroom and returned with a dark mound of fluff in his hands. "This isn't mink, but will it do?"

He dropped a fine black lace shawl about her shoulders. "Oh, Jason," she protested. "I can't borrow this. You shouldn't . . . Whose is it?"

"It's all right, believe me." He tossed her white sweater across the iron railing. "Come on, or we'll be late."

Karaleen hurried out of the house so worried about wearing another woman's shawl that she failed to notice the car in the curving drive until Jason opened its door for her. Instead of the truck, the station wagon, or the jeep, Jason seated Karaleen in a new, luxurious sports car that would have been the envy of any Silicon Valley executive.

"My, your Mr. Arnold has good taste," she murmured.

"Now, don't start worrying about the car," he ordered. "Remember, we're supposed to be having fun."

And they did. The dinner party, a refined but festive affair interrupted by only the briefest of business announcements, was impressive. The country club banquet room was tastefully decorated and the atmosphere pleasant. Except when the conversation centered on unfamiliar agricultural topics, Karaleen felt compatible with most of the local guests. Often she heard Jason's opinion asked, and was surprised at the degree of esteem a ranch manager's position commanded.

Later, leaving the club behind, Karaleen and Jason sailed along the road toward the ranch. The moon's brightness made the headlights seem superfluous. Surrounded by the strains of soft music from the tape deck, Karaleen snuggled into the seat, wrapped in contentment.

She stole a glance at Jason's profile. He was indeed a handsome man with his strong features, broad shoulders, the neat, brown hair. He would make someone a fine husband. What was it he had once said? God hadn't given him the right woman. A simply marvelous husband . . .

Jason broke into her reverie. "What are you thinking about?"

Never would she have told her real thoughts. "You're supposed to say, 'A penny for your thoughts,'" she reproved. Hers had stumbled on a single word, *husband,* and seemed determined to stick there.

"Okay," he began, turning to face her with a warm, dangerous smile. "A penny for—"

"But," Karaleen interrupted, "since you're such a good host, I'll tell you anyway." She ran her fingers along the polished teak wood panels set into the dashboard. "This is a beautiful car."

She concentrated on the feel of the supple leather upholstery, studied the instrument lights—anything to divert her attention from the man sitting next to her, who drove without a trace of nervousness despite the fact that he was barreling along in an expensive borrowed car.

She was the one who was nervous, and began to babble. "I hope you don't get into trouble for borrowing this car." She immediately realized how tactless that remark was as far as Jason's pride was concerned.

He didn't answer.

She tried to make amends. "You know, Jason, a lot of women there tonight would have liked to trade places with me."

"At least with your looks," Jason countered.

"No, with my escort," she said. "Now, don't pretend you didn't notice those admiring glances coming your way all evening." Perfectly aware that her talk was foolish, she bumbled ahead. "Come on, you could have your choice of a number of unattached local belles. Admit it."

She leaned forward to better watch his face. His jaw was firm, his eyes hidden beneath drawn brows. Thinking he was suppressing a grin, she teased on. "I especially noticed that short blonde, the pretty one in the blue dress."

With a suddenness that startled Karaleen, the car braked. It was as if AA-Bee's entrance had caught Jason unaware. The car swerved up the circular drive and squealed to a stop. Almost before the car ceased to rock, Jason was at Karaleen's door. He threw it open and reached toward her. With a firm hold, he yanked her out and imprisoned her, his hands gripping her forearms.

"Don't play games with me!"

Too shocked to protest, she stood helpless, awash in a chilling combination of excitement and alarm. She

118

stared into the dark face above hers. Yes, this was the same man who had been her perfect escort for two days. But the mouth was grim now, the clear eyes narrowed, the handsome face torn by some inner torment. It had to have been her fault. Her idiotic chatter had goaded him into this temper, had touched some hidden nerve.

"I shouldn't have teased. I didn't mean to go too far." She knew nothing of his relationships with any of those women. "It was cruel of me."

His vicelike grip only tightened. The beautiful shawl slid from her shoulders.

"Jason, please," her words slipped between clenched teeth, "you're hurting me."

As if he had been struck, he released her. She teetered toward him and reached to steady herself.

At the feel of his chest, firm and masculine, she snatched her hand away. But, a current running between them, crackling with life, remained.

Her words might have been a recording faintly broadcast from some distant speaker. "I'm sorry, sorry," the recording went, "I wasn't playing games. Sorry . . ."

Suddenly nothing was a game. For Jason's arms were around her. In a hoarse whisper, he breathed. "There was only one woman there tonight that I want."

His hands fastened on her back and crushed her body to his. His mouth came down on hers.

At first Karaleen resisted until, for an immeasurable sweet moment of bliss, she surrendered to an intense physical longing such as she had never before known.

Almost immediately, Jason wrenched himself from her. She dropped back against the car.

Above her own throbbing pulse, she heard Jason's despairing cry. "I shouldn't have done that. Forgive me."

She wanted to shout, *There's nothing to forgive —* wanted to bring him back to her.

Instead she bent and retrieved the shawl, hugging the mound of lace to her breast. It was he who should forgive her. She was not free to accept or return a kiss like that.

Jason berated himself. "I had no right to force myself on you."

"No, don't say that," she commanded with a strength that surprised her. "It was my fault, too. We'll just . . . we'll just forget all about it."

How could she make such an unrealistic proposal? The idea of forgetting that kiss was preposterous. She straightened the new silk dress with quivering hands. "It's over," she tried to sound confident. "Chalk it up to a romantic evening." She folded the shawl neatly over her arm and started toward the house. "And, Jason, this evening was truly one of the nicest I've ever had."

Jason stopped her with a touch. This time it was gentle, and he released her immediately. "I didn't put it well before, but there is only one woman I—"

Her fingers flew to seal his lips. "No!" she cried. "Don't. Please."

Jason stiffened. His face hardened beneath her fingers.

Karaleen drew back. "I . . . I . . ." She must explain, "it isn't you. It's me. I can't make commitments."

Jason caught a savage breath. "Can't? You mean, you *won't*." He spit out the words. "What you're saying is that a hick farmer doesn't fit into your career plans. That's it, isn't it?"

Karaleen bowed her head, blinking back the tears.

Jason waited, long past the time it took for his breathing to slow to normal, for an answer that didn't come.

The moon slipped behind a cloud, erasing the glow of silvery light that had followed them all evening. When it returned, Jason had disappeared.

The next morning Karaleen sat in the living room dreading Jason's appearance. No words were exchanged when he arrived. Like a robot she carried her briefcase and the new dress packed in its box, and followed Jason as he took her suitcase to the station wagon.

They drove in silence to the white clapboard church. Jason, his tanned face looking drawn, politely shared his Bible whenever the Scriptures were cited. Karaleen's eyes dutifully followed the words, but her mind dwelled on Jason's question, *Where does God fit into your plans?* Her interest in the sermon was a shameful pretense.

Jason closed his Bible and stood for the final hymn. Embossed on its brown cover was the outline of a dove. That was it! Jason had seen the dove on her bumper sticker when they first met. At that time, the symbol and its message, *The Way,* meant nothing to her, but from that, Jason would have assumed that she was a Christian, the kind of Christian Rosalie was.

Immediately after church, Karaleen hurried outside. He followed and drove her directly to the airstrip. He helped Chuck ready the plane while Karaleen stood quietly by.

As Karaleen boarded, Jason handed her a black zippered portfolio. "These papers should supply everything you need for the job."

Even before the plane left the ground, Jason's station wagon roared away from the airstrip and went speeding down the road in the direction of the AA-Bee Citrus Ranch.

CHAPTER 8

ALTHOUGH KARALEEN HAD SLEPT little the night before, she took special pains with her clothes and make up so that, on Monday morning when she walked into Vali-Turf's South County office, she felt close to her old self. Ringing telephones, the brisk tapping of a printwheel, a file drawer gliding shut—all combined to give her the feeling of being back on track. Here, in such an atmosphere, a person knew his role. No, it wasn't Silicon Valley, but Lester's branch office had become a second home to Karaleen. She even managed a cheery greeting for Thelma.

Karaleen put her briefcase on the credenza behind her desk, gave its smooth leather a loving pat, and walked to the private door between her office and Lester's. There was a certain high-priority item that needed to be resolved. It was time to get her personal life on line.

At her knock, Lester called an invitation. She slipped over and closed Lester's outer door, which led to the hallway. Without a word she swiveled his chair away from his desk and plopped down on his lap.

"Miss me?" Her arms stole over the blush that rose in his neck. "No, don't look at the door. It's locked."

Lester broke into a hearty laugh. "You little flirt."

Karaleen sat perfectly still as Lester's lips neared. His kiss was tentative, then firm, then hard. She responded in kind until, her eyes still open, a sales graph on the wall came into focus, its black line climbing in absolute parallel with the intensity of Lester's kiss.

Karaleen disentangled herself and scrambled to her feet. Lester grabbed for her, but she planted herself firmly just out of his reach and crossed her arms.

Lester contented himself with a slow, thorough inspection of her from head to toe, a pleased smile on his face. "You're looking mighty sharp this morning. New dress?"

"What? This old thing?" she cried in an exaggerated tone. "You've seen it a dozen times." She shook her finger, "But wait until you feast your eyes on my weekend purchase. Now, there's a new new dress that's really a new dress."

He tried again to pull her into his lap. "I can hardly wait."

"To see my dress?" she teased and backed away.

"That, too," he grinned. "But I doubt that the dress in any way measures up to the beauty of its owner."

"I hope you feel the same after my expense report crosses your desk."

"Oh? Wear it for me tonight," he begged. "We'll go someplace special. How about the Bay Club?"

She tilted her head and considered. "Well, the Bay Club might be good enough."

"Must be some dress."

"I told you. Thelma's calculator is going to short-circuit."

Lester laughed. "As long as it did the job. Were all those rich growers properly appreciative?"

Karaleen stiffened.

"Now, honey," Lester said quickly, "don't misinterpret. I just meant . . . after all, Vali-Turf has to make a good impression." He winked, "Of course, certain of our employees would make a good impression dressed in rags, scanty rags."

"Lester!"

"I'm sorry, it just popped out. I can't help it if your pretty little face makes me forget you're a topnotch programmer, to say nothing of your gorgeous—"

"Oh?" Karaleen raised her eyebrows. "How would you feel if I told you that your precious potential customers up in citrus country forgot all about my programming talents?"

Lester bolted to his feet and engulfed her in a bear hug. "The next grower's dinner might find the hamburger laced with ground-up floppy disks." He backed off and eyed her warily, "Maybe it's time you turned in a detailed trip report."

Karaleen hoped that her laugh sounded more natural to Lester than it did to her. "Only if I give it orally and we're not bugged for sound." She gravely inspected the penholder on Lester's desk and peeked beneath his calendar. Then she opened her eyes wide and began confidentially, "You've heard about the virile, outdoor type?"

Lester shook her gently. "Hush, that's enough teasing. I've got to finish checking this proposal. Get out of here so I can get some work done."

Karaleen started away, but suddenly she turned and faced Lester from the opposite side of his desk. His head was already bowed over a myriad of papers.

"Lester," her voice arched across the space between them, "let's announce our engagement—*now*."

Lester's fingers traced a path across columns of figures, the other hand marking a place on the left margin of a stack of printout sheets. Karaleen noticed how thick his hands were, in keeping with the rest of his muscular body. When his finger reached the last column, it fell over the edge and began to idly flip the rough perforated edges.

"I thought we agreed," he reminded softly, "that it might be best to wait a while."

"How long, Lester?" Her head felt strangely light. She leaned against the desk.

He tapped the edges of the printout sheets against the desktop until they were perfectly stacked. "We have our jobs to consider. If we're careful, we can both come out of this in good shape. No repercussions. No office romance gossip."

Karaleen's mouth was dry. "How do you plan to get married without any rumors of romance?"

"Hey, now," Lester scolded, and shot her a meaningful glance, "we've got our romance all right." The glance traveled downward from her face. "It's just that we're not going to lose our perspective."

"But, Lester," Karaleen straightened, her palms rotating against one another in a slow circle. "This isn't like a real engagement. Sometimes, I almost forget . . ."

Lester bounded around the desk and threw one arm over her shoulders. The other hand tipped her face toward his. "Tell you what. I had thought it would be wise to wait until you were finished down here and were safely back in the home office. Then, any speculation would be hindsight." He caressed her face. "Now, don't look away. I've just changed my mind. We'll make the big announcement on Friday. Okay?"

"Why Friday?"

Lester kissed the tip of her nose. "Because I can't wait any longer." He nuzzled her neck. "Besides, we're having a party Friday anyway. The Ortega job winds up."

Karaleen let him kiss her briefly on the mouth.

125

"Five o'clock Friday," Lester murmured. "Now," he turned her and shoved gently, "go away and let me get myself back in gear."

In her office, Karaleen flipped the desk calendar over to Friday and wrote, *Party* opposite the five o'clock time slot.

Upon opening her briefcase, the first thing she found was the black portfolio that Jason had given her just before takeoff the day before. She threw it in the back of a file drawer and slammed the drawer shut. Lester's promise to make public their engagement on Friday had restored order to her life. But she didn't need reminders of the weekend to cloud the issue. She would work on the AA-Bee Citrus Project—if indeed there was such a project—when her fingers ceased to tremble at the touch of a few informational sheets.

By early afternoon, she had cleared her desk and prepared to tackle the inhouse job of computerizing the sales program. She buzzed Thelma, intending to set up a meeting when they could go over some figures together.

Thelma responded tersely, "I have a deadline to meet."

Karaleen sighed inwardly and resisted the urge to reply that everyone had deadlines to meet. Instead she tried to tactfully ignore the negative answer. "You just name the time. I'll be there whenever you say."

"I must prepare a customer mailing so the girls can get it out this week," Thelma said flatly. "I'm afraid that will take most of my time the next few days."

Once again frustrated and impatient, Karaleen resorted to working around the problem, digging out such information as she was able.

At the apartment that night, Karaleen came out of her room dressed in the shimmering forest green silk. She opened her mouth to ask Rosalie if her slip was showing or if the hem was unraveling. Something just didn't feel right.

"Ooh," Rosalie breathed, "that kind of dress calls for a dozen roses and moonlight and a proposal. Watch out."

Karaleen whirled back to the bedroom, tore the zipper open, and dropped the dress to the floor. She stepped out of the fragile heap, and opened the closet.

"A single rose was more than enough," she muttered.

When Lester picked her up, he looked quizzically at the plain brown wool she wore. "Nice," he remarked weakly.

"Oh," Karaleen said, "I decided to save the biggie." She swept ahead of him down the steps. "I'll dazzle you with it on a really special occasion."

Rosalie called after them, "Karaleen, don't forget to ask Lester about tomorrow night."

In the car Lester inquired, "What about tomorrow night?"

"Well," Karaleen paused, not sure how to broach the subject. Rosalie would have just plunged in. "You know Rosalie and Rick always invite me to their Tuesday night Bible study. Tomorrow night it's going to be at Rosalie's apartment." She turned anxiously to Lester. "Please come, Lester. I'd really like you to."

"Oh, I don't know," Lester began.

"It's kind of important to me. I mean, we've never even talked about how each of us feels about—"

"We can do that sometime. Sure, it's important that we get into some deep discussions. But, don't you think we need a more private setting for that than an apartment full of people?"

"Maybe, but this Bible study is interesting. I've been a few times. It's a pretty intellectual group. Of course," she added quickly, "the purpose isn't just to analyze the Scriptures, but to learn from them."

"Oh, I'm not entirely a stranger to Bible stories, Karaleen. But this is a busy week."

The car eased into a parking space at the Bay Club. As Lester helped Karaleen out, she said, "With such a big change coming up in our lives," and she drew Lester's hand to her lips briefly, "I need to make sure I've got my head on straight. Lately," and she leaned gratefully against him, "I seem to be questioning a lot of things—things that before I was either positive about or ignored completely. I guess I feel I have some growing to do in my spiritual life." Arm in arm, they walked toward the Bay Club entrance. "I was hoping we could do some searching and some growing together."

"Sure we will, darling."

The next afternoon as Karaleen left work, she stopped in Lester's office to repeat Rosalie's invitation.

"Next time." He stretched and spread his arms over his cluttered desk. "I won't be able to get away from here for hours. You pay close attention, and tell me all about it." He gave her a furtive kiss with one eye on the open office door.

The discussion that night was on the subject of love and marriage. Even with her Bible open to the sixth chapter of Second Corinthians, Karaleen felt as she often did in these studies, grossly inadequate in Bible knowledge and half afraid to voice questions.

After everyone was gone, she asked Rosalie, "What was that about not being bound together with an unbeliever?"

"Some versions say not to be 'unequally yoked.' " Rosalie seemed to read Karaleen's mind and explained, "I feel certain this includes marriage. Especially marriage."

"You're telling me that a believer shouldn't marry an unbeliever?"

Rosalie nodded firmly.

That night Karaleen prayed that Lester would come with her to the next week's study.

The middle of the week, Karaleen began work on the AA-Bee Citrus job. As she had suspected, it was quite simple. After going over the information from Jason, she decided the proposal would include only a microcomputer and purchased packages of software. There was no need for custom programming work, even though a look at the gross receipts told Karaleen the operation was much bigger than she had surmised.

One thing puzzled her. Jason had taken pains to include copies of reports on every phase of the corporation's activities. There were tax figures, depreciation schedules, production reports, operating expenses; but the data was sketchy in one area—payroll. She should have it before completing the proposal, but because she was recommending prewritten programs, she would just figure in the payroll software she deemed best and be prepared with an alternate. Actually, she was surprised that Jason had done as well as he had in compiling this information.

She met with Lester early Friday morning for review of the week's work. She pulled out the AA-Bee Citrus proposal package, but before she could begin, Lester stopped her.

"Hold off on that, Karaleen. We're kind of rushed for time this morning. Harry wants to keep close tabs on that one. So why don't you just give him a call? No need to go over it with me. I trust your judgment."

"Why is Harry so interested?"

"I guess he has high hopes for ag sales in the Central Valley. He may be right, but at the present, the ag market doesn't show me much. The action is either down here or up at Silicon Valley."

The next item was Karaleen's inhouse job.

"Good gosh!" Lester exclaimed. "Still sitting on that?"

Karaleen bit her lip and drummed her pencil on the papers before her. She saw red every time she looked at Thelma. She didn't need any flak from Lester. "It's been difficult to dig out everything I need."

"But I told Harry this was nearly done."

Karaleen said evenly, "I wasn't aware of any deadline on this job."

"Well, there wasn't an exact deadline. It was more of an estimate."

"In that case," Karaleen prepared to close the folder. "I'll continue as I have, working on it between other jobs."

"Except . . ." Lester twisted in his chair. He toyed with a paperweight and set it down hard. "Harry is expecting me to tell him we're ready to go on line in two weeks."

Karaleen jumped to her feet. "What?"

"So you can see," Lester said, "we'd better get cracking on it."

"Now wait a minute," Karaleen said. "How did you arrive at a completion date of two weeks? What about consulting the Senior Programmer in charge of the job?"

Lester frowned. "You mean that estimate didn't clear your desk?" His face flamed and he half rose. "I'll choke that Thelma."

Of course, Karaleen thought, Thelma routinely prepared brief weekly summaries of all the manpower estimates, but only *after* she had obtained the estimates from the proper people. Karaleen tried not to believe that this was another attempt on Thelma's part to make her life miserable. But what else could she think? With an effort, she tried to conceal her anger. "At least, it's not a customer's job. We'll just explain to Harry that the target date was off."

"Explain," Lester spit out the word as if it had a nasty taste. "This office doesn't make mistakes unless there's an excellent reason." He passed a hand through his blond hair. "And there is one!" He brightened. "A valid one that should satisfy Harry. You've simply been spending so much time on his baby, that ag stuff, that you are going to have to slip your completion date on the inhouse work."

"*My* completion date! I don't know . . ." Karaleen began.

Lester stood up and drew on his coat. "I'll talk to Harry about it. In the meantime, you call him and report on that citrus thing. That'll keep him happy." Lester straightened his tie. "Don't worry, sweetie," he leaned close, "Harry thinks you can do no wrong." He was out the door, calling over his shoulder, "Be back after lunch."

In her office, Karaleen spread the AA-Bee Citrus work on her desk. She stared from the telephone to the penciled figures and back to the telephone. Harry had always been up front with her, and she didn't like being a part of any scheme to deceive him, even one as minor as glossing over an error.

She picked up the receiver. Well, she could talk to him about Mr. Arnold's citrus ranch. That was honest. Maybe she could change Lester's mind about the other.

"Lester said you wanted a personal update on the AA-Bee Citrus project," she told Harry, and launched into her appraisal of the operation's needs.

When she mentioned the payroll situation, Harry brushed it off with, "No problem. You can get it straight from the source when you deliver the package."

Karaleen thought there might be a bad connection. "What did you say?"

"When you deliver the proposal. I've been in contact with Arnold. As a matter of fact, he called not five minutes ago. He'd like to see you tomorrow. Does that fit your schedule?"

"Tomorrow? Saturday? Harry, what are you talking about? There's no reason why I can't drop this in the mail. He'll have it Monday morning."

"I know you worked last weekend. Look, this Arnold is pretty insistent. He wants you to bring everything up to him. He wants a personal presentation. And he came on strong about tomorrow. I was just preparing to call you."

Karaleen's heart fell. She must talk Harry out of this insane idea. "Look, I don't know what kind of line this man is feeding you, but this job is not as big as you think. It's all packaged software! I know he's worth bucks, but how much computer stuff can one farming business use? Besides, I . . ." the words caught in her throat. Harry was proposing another weekend of facing Jason Bradley.

Despite her dismay at that prospect, a sudden wry thought intrigued her. With Jason's boss on the premises, things might be different—yes, quite different. It would be interesting to see how free Mr. Arnold really was with the keys to his fancy car.

But interesting as the situation sounded, nothing could warrant meeting Jason again. She had worked hard the past week to regroup her emotions. She was back on course now.

"I want you to know how much I appreciate this," Harry was still talking. "Take a company car if you'd rather. I'll tell him you'll be there late morning. Be careful now."

"Harry, weren't you listening?" Karaleen broke in. "I can't go." But Harry had hung up.

"No, no," Karaleen murmured, dropping her head in her hands. "I just can't."

Her eyes fell on the daily calendar before her. Opposite five o'clock, she read, *Party*. Her back jerked ramrod straight. "Of course, I can," she told herself. After five o'clock that afternoon, she would be a different person. Nothing—no one—would throw her into an upheaval such as the turmoil she had felt the previous weekend. At five o'clock, she and Lester would announce publicly that they were engaged to be married.

The receptionist had made arrangements for a private room at a nearby restaurant. The entire South

County organization was invited, and Karaleen could feel the undercurrent of anticipation well before time for the office to close.

At four, Lester asked her to come into his office. With both doors shut, she went to him. "In a little while we can yell it from the rooftops," she said softly.

He kissed her long and hard. She closed her eyes and let herself concentrate on the pleasure of being wrapped in his steady arms. "We'll have a good life," she whispered, "Mr. and Mrs. Lester Peterson."

"Wonder-man and wonder-wife," he laughed shakily, "technologically speaking."

She snickered, "You make us sound like some kind of bionic couple."

"Be quiet and kiss me again," he ordered.

His lips moved from her mouth, over her face, and rested in her dark hair. "It's hard to be patient," he said, his voice thick.

"We don't have to be for long." Karaleen fingered the smooth silk of Lester's tie. "Lester," she said suddenly, "let's set the date. Let's don't stop at a mere announcement. Let's go ahead and issue the invitations."

Lester held her slightly apart. "What an impetuous fool I'm involved with," he teased.

"I'm serious. We can at least set the month—say June? We can call my parents tonight and everybody else that matters. I'll start making arrangements, and we'll zero in on a definite date. Won't Harry be surprised? Of course, we'll have to see about getting ourselves assigned to work in the same end of the state. Unless," she laughed, "we want a commuter marriage."

She stopped abruptly at the look on Lester's face.

"Hey, there," he cautioned, "slow down and let me catch up." He half shrugged and squeezed her playfully. "Don't you think one earth-shaking announcement at a time is enough?"

Karaleen pushed back in Lester's embrace. His arms were no longer warm and comforting; they had become cold, steely bars. "You said," her words squeaked out tiny and shivery, "I thought you were anxious."

"Of course, I am." His lips sought hers, but she turned her face. "You don't know how anxious."

Lester was a brilliant, logical person. Why weren't his words making sense?

"I'm only thinking of our position with the company," he continued. "Right now seems an inopportune time to give the impression that we may have been more involved in personal matters than in our work, especially because I was the one who requested your assignment here. And now this slippage on the inhouse stuff."

The bars across Karaleen's back tightened. It might have been a hug.

"I mean," the wizard from the South County office talked on, "we can probably get by with announcing our engagement, but rushing—"

She broke out of the bars as if they were toothpicks. Crossing the room she flung open the door to her office, but stopped herself by catching hold of the doorframe with both hands. Only when the pain in her fingers became so acute that she felt it over the pain that threatened to tear open her chest did she realize that her fingernails had dug into the wood.

"Lester." Surely Karaleen thought, such a cool prim voice did not come from her, the girl with the bleeding nails. "I believe our engagement was an error." What a strange thing someone was saying. "Therefore, let us delete it from our files and from our memories."

Karaleen closed her ears to Lester's objections and then closed the door on his words about remaining friends.

That night, crying into her pillow, Karaleen relived

once again the scene in Lester's office. Except this time, she remembered clearly the ridiculous pronouncement she had made as she broke the engagement. A long, hysterical giggle interrupted her sobs. Then, the giggle still on her lips, she dropped into a peaceful sleep.

On Saturday morning, Karaleen drove toward the Central Valley, amazed that, as the sun rose in the sky, so did her spirits rise. *No one would believe,* she thought to herself, *that less than twenty-four hours before she had dis-engaged herself from an attractive, promising young executive who wanted them to marry and honeymoon their way up the corporate ladder.*

She couldn't be too angry with Lester. She was sure he did love her in his own way, and he had suggested an arrangement that he thought would benefit both of them. His priorities were askew, that was all.

The road sloped down to the wide valley floor. Karaleen passed a few oil rigs. She was less successful at identifying the irrigated row crops and green fields. At the first sight of citrus, the car leaped ahead until she had to make herself slow down.

In the matter of Lester, she was not without guilt. She had gone along with him, even suspecting that her heart was not in complete agreement with her head.

She sighed. At least she could once again point her personal plans in a single direction. She would still have a fine career in Silicon Valley, and she would earn it all on her own. She had done all right so far, hadn't she? She thought warmly of Harry's regard for her, and of her reputation as a good programmer.

The road became a two-lane corridor between lush citrus groves. She slowed, glancing at the map on the seat beside her. She would have no trouble controlling her topsy-turvy feelings in the presence of that ranch manager now that her life was back on course. *After yesterday*, she thought, turning into the circular drive

135

of the AA-Bee Citrus property, and stopping before the sprawling Spanish home, *I can handle anything*.

The grounds seemed deserted. Of course, with Mr. Arnold in residence, Jason would not likely be lounging around the house. She relished the rich atmosphere of the pleasant veranda as she rang the bell.

Genevieve opened the door, a wide smile on her face. "Come in, come in."

Karaleen stepped into the polished entry hall. "How nice to see you again, Genevieve."

Genevieve led the way into the living room. "Everyone is scattered. Make yourself comfortable."

Karaleen set her briefcase on the plush carpet. She sank into a comfortable chair facing the patio, but the rooms aroused bittersweet feelings in her. She flipped through a news magazine, put it down, and walked around. She had stopped to admire an especially beautiful philodendron when a familiar tone sent her pulse racing.

"Miss Hammonds?" How formal Jason was today. She turned slowly.

For a brief moment, she thought the man before her really was Jason. But this neatly-dressed gentleman was much older. Even though he bore a warm look amazingly similar to that of the ranch manager, it bothered her that she was beginning to see Jason Bradley even when he was not present.

"Yes, I'm Karaleen Hammonds."

The man stared at her much as she must have stared at him. He caught himself, "Forgive me, it's just that I've heard a great deal about you. I'm afraid I was overly curious to see how closely my mental image paralleled the real person."

In the exchange of pleasantries regarding Karaleen's drive and the weather, she began to relax. There really was a Mr. Arnold, and he was aware that Vali-Turf was proposing computer equipment for his citrus business. Jason must have discussed the idea with his employer.

"Is your luggage still in your car?" he asked.

"Yes," Karaleen acknowledged, but quickly added, "I plan to get a room in town, or if we finish early enough, I'll start back tonight."

The tall gentleman dismissed her plans with a wave of the hand. "We wouldn't think of letting you drive back tonight, and we certainly can't send you to a motel. I'll get your bag."

Karaleen followed him to the car protesting, "Really, I just can't impose on you."

He waited for her to open the car trunk. She fumbled with the keys, trying to think of a way to gracefully refuse. This strictly business trip was about to become complicated.

Suddenly, a startled look crossed the man's face, and he reddened as if embarrassed. "My *wife* will insist that you be our guest." He looked toward the house. "She should be out any minute."

His effort to reassure her that his was an honorable suggestion was touching and yet so obvious that Karaleen bent over the trunk latch to hide her amusement. No wonder that Harry wanted to please this considerate man. How could she insult him by refusing his hospitality? Besides, she might not even see the ranch manager now that the owner was here to answer his own questions.

That thought, coupled with her host's graciousness, added a spring to Karaleen's walk as she returned to the house.

"You don't know what a pleasure it is for me to be able to enjoy your beautiful home." She stepped into the entry. "I've drooled over these lovely Spanish-style houses ever since I came to California. I certainly never thought I'd be staying . . ."

Her voice trailed away. She had resolved to act naturally and with no undue concern in any contact

137

with the AA-Bee Citrus ranch manager. But now, Jason Bradley stood waiting in the living room, and at the sight of him, her good intentions deserted her.

He looked different. Gone were the dusty boots, replaced by white leather casual shoes that might have been at home in a Palm Springs Country Club.

Steadying herself on the black iron railing, Karaleen stepped down into the living room. She smiled carefully at Jason and began again, "I never thought—"

"What she means is," Jason's icy words stabbed like knives, "she thought that we hick farmers lived in one-room cabins and locked our wives in the root cellars on Saturday night while we went off to town and whooped it up."

From somewhere, Karaleen heard a sudden outcry—her own. During the excruciating silence that followed, she stared at the handsome man poised casually near the fireplace. Soon he would laugh. Surely his words were some kind of cruel joke, too cruel to have been uttered by the Jason Bradley she knew.

A new presence entered. "Now, Jason," a petite gray-haired woman cautioned and then murmured in Karaleen's direction, "Never mind, dear, he's been edgy lately."

Karaleen located the leather briefcase by the chair where she had left it. She would snatch it up, grab her suitcase from Mr. Arnold's hand, and escape this make-believe scene.

Now the older man spoke up. "Where are our manners?" he asked. "Anna, let me introduce you to Karaleen Hammonds. Miss Hammonds, may I present my wife, Anna Bradley?"

"How do you do, Mrs. . . ." the name caught in Karaleen's throat, burning there until she was barely able to repeat it, ". . .Bradley?"

Karaleen whirled toward the fireplace to find Jason

wearing a look of utter and complete triumph. "I don't understand," she said. "Are . . . ?"

He kept his distance, dispatching a cool voice to finish her thought, "Yes, Anna and Arnold Bradley are my parents."

CHAPTER 9

"WELL, OF COURSE, SHE'S aware that we're your parents . . ." Arnold Bradley began, but stopped, his words hanging in midair. He addressed Karaleen, "You did know Jason is my son as well as being the ranch manager?" A sharp glance at Karaleen's confused expression and an even sharper one toward Jason gave him his answer. "I must apologize if there's been a misunderstanding."

"No, no," Karaleen interjected. She did not know what was going on, but she couldn't let this kind man take the blame. "I seem to have gotten the wrong impression."

Jason's mother shook her head. "Jason has talked incessantly about you, my dear. Didn't he tell you he's as much the owner of this ranch as we are? Arnold and I spend most of the winter at our house in town, and the summer on the coast, now that he's practically taken over."

"It's all right, Mother," Jason spoke up. "Ms. Hammonds and I failed to communicate well on several matters. She has her own idea of life on the farm, and it in no way compares with the glamour of a career in the world of high technology. I tried my best to sway her opinion, but she wouldn't listen. And I'm sure nothing, not even the responsibilities and,'' he paused dramatically, ''the *rewards* of running an agricultural operation like this can change her mind.''

As if he had thrown a gauntlet, Jason had challenged her. No, it was more than a challenge. There could be no answer to his tirade. Karaleen's thoughts rushed back to the last evening they had spent together, when they had parted with his angry assertion that she would never let a hick farmer fit into her plans. Now it was as if this arrogant stranger with steel in his eyes and a knife in his words had just announced, *You didn't want me as a hick farmer. Well, this farmer happens to be a big-time operator. You should have jumped when you had the chance, because any move you make now will look like fortune-hunting.*

Never in Karaleen's life had she felt so mortified. She wished that Jason had strode across the room and hit her, that he had knocked her mercifully unconscious. But, no, she was alert, heart pounding, keenly aware of three pairs of eyes focused upon her. She should say something diplomatic but she couldn't say anything at all.

Mr. Bradley cleared his throat uncomfortably. ''Yes, well. Anna, why don't you take Miss Hammonds to her room? She can freshen up before lunch.''

Karaleen was aware of Mrs. Bradley gently propelling her down the hall. As they went, she heard Mr. Bradley's terse comment, ''I suppose there was an excellent reason behind that assault.''

In the green and white bedroom, Mrs. Bradley straightened a picture on the wall. She checked the bathroom twice, and pointed out where extra towels were stored. She seemed reluctant to leave, torn between trying to atone for a mysterious unpleasant moment and her obvious loyalty to her son. Before closing the door, she said, so like a mother that another time Karaleen would have smiled, "Jason is usually such a polite person."

The table in the dining room was set for four. Mr. Bradley seated his wife and Karaleen, saying that Jason had been called to the field on a maintenance problem.

She and Mr. Bradley spent the afternoon in the office, Mr. Bradley explaining that Jason was tied up and they would go ahead without him.

Karaleen reviewed the proposal in detail. She was surprised at the depth of Mr. Bradley's questions. His interest extended beyond the simple packaged programs she was suggesting.

"Let's talk about what you could do for me if I should plan to do my own shipping, for instance?" he said.

She answered his questions, glad to immerse herself in a familiar topic with a layman who seemed able to grasp any concept she threw at him.

When she heard a clock strike five, she brought the session to a close and began to pack her briefcase. She would withdraw gracefully and leave the AA-Bee Citrus Ranch, which she had discovered had received it's name from Anna and Arnold years before Jason reached the age of participating. The "Bee" stood for Bradley, and that took care of Jason's last name, if not his first.

"Mr. Bradley," she said, "We've done all that's necessary. If you'll excuse me, I'll get my things and be on my way after I've said goodbye to Mrs. Bradley.

"Nonsense," he boomed.

Despite his protest, she hurried on, "I appreciate your hospitality, but I have to leave."

"No, you must stay. We're having guests tonight

142

for a barbecue. You'd be an asset to the group. Everyone is interested in computers." He leaned over confidentially, "It's the *in* topic, you know."

Against her better judgment, but swayed by her host's graciousness and the unattractive alternative of a long drive after dark, Karaleen consented to stay.

To her surprise, the evening with the Bradleys and three other families was pleasant. She had already met one of the ladies at the growers' dinner. Also, she couldn't help being flattered at the attention given her as she answered questions plied by the guests. Most of the inquiries were general, but one man was interested in computerizing a feedlot operation.

She tried to respond with more animation than she felt, to show that she was over the hurt Jason had dealt. She focused intensely on those about her, ignoring Jason, who hung on the edge of the conversation, strangely subdued.

Several guests were teenagers. From where Karaleen sat in the living room after dinner, she could see the brick patio. The outside lights clicked off. Two shadowy figures moved toward each other. Karaleen watched the gleam of white arms raise to meet a quick embrace.

She suddenly felt old and oddly alone. She shrugged off such a silly response. Curious to see if either mother had noticed the couple, she surveyed the room and caught sight of Jason. He, too, had a clear view of the scene on the patio, but shifted his gaze to her. Their eyes met and held until she turned away from the strange mixture of pain and longing in his.

Casually, she made her way to her hostess. "It's been a long day for me," she apologized, "I hope you won't mind if I excuse myself before your guests leave."

Karaleen slipped into her room and drew the drapes across the sliding door that led to the patio. Even though she lay awake for hours, she did not stir from her room. Not in a thousand years would she risk a private meeting with Jason. He would never be able to call her "fortune hunter."

The following morning, Jason did not appear for breakfast. Karaleen packed her things and drove behind Mr. and Mrs. Bradley to the same church she had attended with Jason. No explanation was made of Jason's absence, and after church, Karaleen took her leave.

Karaleen drove along the deserted two-lane road, relieved to be on her way and in the knowledge that she need never again enter that beautiful Spanish house with its uncanny way of turning her life upside down.

Mr. Bradley had given her explicit directions on how to reach the highway leading south. There was only one turn. She executed it and then accelerated on the straightway.

Suddenly she realized that something was amiss on the road ahead. Her first thought was of an accident, but as she slowed and drew near, she saw that a truck was parked across the lane on her side of the road. Immediately her concern changed to alarm at the sight of the familiar man striding purposefully toward her.

Her impulse was to throw the car into gear and flee. She resisted. This man was not going to upset her any longer. She would treat him with the courtesy due a business contact because that was what he was—nothing more.

Jason waited as she rolled down the window. He leaned both hands on the door, his face above her eye level. Traces of fine hair on the backs of his strong, rough hands were visible in the bright sun. Her mind went to their first meeting on a lonely country road.

Unable to stand the silence, she took the offensive. "Do you need a tow-truck or anything?"

He bent his face to the window. She flinched at the strain it showed. Even his eyes, staring at some distant point, were lifeless and their color seemed to have paled.

He spoke. "Once again, I owe you an apology."

"Don't." She wanted only to forget it.

"Yesterday . . . I'm sorry."

It was the first time she had known him not to look her straight in the eyes when he spoke.

"I lashed out at you, embarrassed you, all because I had read into our times together something that wasn't there. No," he rushed on as she tried to stop him, "let me explain. You see, I thought I could convince you my kind of life wasn't so bad. I had even begun to think I was cracking your resistance." His nails gripping the door were edged with white. "Then, when you rejected me that night after the dinner I was hurt, and I decided to make you hurt just as much. I could hardly wait to get you back here so I could cut you down. You don't know how carefully I engineered that meeting."

"Jason." Just to say the name was a struggle. "Stop."

His hand moved inside the car until his fingers touched her shoulder, lightly, as if asking permission to be there.

She clung to the wheel. "I'm leaving now. Let's just forget it ever happened."

But Jason continued, "I don't know what there is about you that brings out the worst in me. I was boorish. No, worse than that. Cruel."

The rein that had kept her anger under control since meeting Jason the day before burst. "Now you're blaming it on me!" she cried, tears stinging her eyes.

His fingers grasped at her shoulder until she winced. Immediately he released her. "No, I—"

"Not only did you humiliate me yesterday, but you deceived me all along. And the reason for that is obvious. You were afraid that if I knew you were more than a hired hand, I'd snatch you up because of your money."

"No, Karaleen, you're wrong. You made the assumption that I only worked on the ranch. I let you keep thinking that because I was afraid if you knew I owned land and that I was here to stay, you'd write me off without ever giving me a chance."

"Sure," she retorted, "You made it perfectly clear yesterday in your little show that anyone interested in you is a fortune-hunter. Well, I don't need your fortune, and I don't need you."

There, she plunged the sword straight in to Jason's heart and twisted it. His face, gray and hard as stone, drew back from the window. Arms straight, their veins throbbing, he leaned against the car and bowed his head between his arms.

Karaleen couldn't see his face, only the thick brown hair. She grabbed a tissue from the seat beside her and swabbed at the tears streaming down her face.

She had to get away. In a quick motion, she turned the ignition key. She drew deep, shuddering breaths in time with the motor, racing and then settling into a uneasy rhythm.

"Goodbye, Jason," she said flatly. The car began to roll. His hands dropped away. She swerved into the open lane around his truck and drove on toward South County, carrying with her the greatest burden of sadness she had ever known.

On Monday morning, Lester greeted Karaleen as if there had never been an engagement. Once or twice during the days that followed Karaleen glanced from her work to find Lester staring at her. He looked away as quickly as she did, and neither made reference to their personal relationship.

She wished that her dealings with Thelma could have been as smooth, and thought how ironic it was that she could behave more naturally with a former fiancé than she could with the office manager.

One of Thelma's duties was to collect information from several sources and estimate future sales figures.

These forecasts were an important factor in determining the productivity of the South County office.

Karaleen's was to set up a new system whereby all the information would be fed into a computer program that would then make projected sales forecast. The forecast could be changed on a moment-by-moment basis simply by feeding into the computer any new bit of information. The change would ripple through all the figures, giving end results that would be accurate and up-to-date.

"But Thelma," Karaleen told the office manager one day when she was finally able to corner her, "if I knew what has been done in the past, it would help establish a realistic formula for sales projections."

Thelma, with her usual birdlike jerking movements, opened a file drawer. She pulled out several thick folders. "You're asking for the sort of know-how that isn't written down in black and white. Here."

Karaleen flipped through the folders. "This looks like labor schedules for a power company program."

"It is," Thelma said, as if surprised that Karaleen was able to read.

Later, in her office, Karaleen found that the files consisted only of labor schedules for a program that had been cancelled before its completion. None of the information Karaleen had requested was there.

Another invincible wall. Karaleen gritted her teeth, dreaming of the day Thelma would get her comeuppance.

Almost before Karaleen realized it, two weeks passed. How glad she would be to return to northern California, back to her own apartment and some sort of normal social life. Rosalie saw to it that Karaleen met several "eligible" young men, but nothing materialized beyond the first double date and casual conversations at the Bible study or at church.

"You're not interested, are you, Karaleen?" Rosalie asked. "You aren't holding out on me, are you? 'Fess up. You're secretly engaged."

147

Karaleen laughed. "I'm sorry, I guess it's that I'm too unsettled now to get involved with anyone. I won't be in the area much longer, I hope." She caught herself. "Oh, Rosalie, I didn't mean that the way it sounded. You know how much I like being with you. It's just that I don't feel as if I belong down here, living out of a suitcase, working on a temporary assignment. Besides, you and Rick will be married soon. Then I'll really be lost."

One morning the receptionist appeared at Karaleen's office and announced a visitor, a Mr. Bradley.

Karaleen was just replacing the telephone receiver. She fumbled, and it clattered to the floor.

The receptionist giggled, "Goodness, I didn't mean to upset you. He seems a nice gentleman, sort of fatherly. I don't think he'll bite."

So relieved to know that it was the elder Mr. Bradley, Karaleen hurried to the lobby and greeted him warmly.

"I had business down your way," he explained as she showed him her office, "and thought perhaps you'd have lunch with a lonely traveler."

"How nice of you to think of me," she said. "I'd love to, but you must be my guest this time." She wondered if he would object to a woman picking up the tab as his son had. Evidently not, for he smiled and nodded, and went on to comment about the freeway traffic.

"Let me bring you up to date on the AA-Bee Citrus job," she suggested, "but first, I'd like you to meet Mr. Peterson, our branch manager."

Lester exhibited his most gracious behavior for Mr. Bradley. "You know, Mr. Bradley, Karaleen is our top person when it comes to programming." He walked near Karaleen's chair, letting his hand rest on her shoulder.

Karaleen was conscious that Lester's touch was not missed by Mr. Bradley, who sat near her desk thoughtfully tapping a silver pen on a pocket notepad. She shifted forward over her desk, so that Lester moved his hand, skimming over her back and into his pocket.

At lunch Mr. Arnold guided the conversation along personal lines, more so than Karaleen liked. But, she did nothing to rebuke him. As he had in his home, he gave her the impression of genuine interest and respect.

He commented on the office set-up and on Lester. "Mr. Peterson seems a capable person."

Karaleen continued, "He's known as the whiz-kid of Vali-Turf." Then, hoping he wouldn't consider her attitude toward the branch manager too flippant, she added, "He's really a competent manager. The company is fortunate to have him."

"And I think he feels fortunate to have you."

Karaleen blushed. "Oh, he was exaggerating."

"I believe he appreciates you," Mr. Bradley paused and added with a wink, "perhaps in more ways than one?"

The comment took Karaleen by such surprise, that she gasped out without thinking, "Not now. It's all over."

She stopped, horrified that she had tacitly agreed with Mr. Bradley's assessment of Lester's feelings. She had to explain such a stupid remark, "I mean," she searched for words, and then came out with the truth. "We were engaged, but only for a short while. As a matter of fact," she hurried on, more and more agitated, "I . . . we called it off the day before I drove up to your ranch. I don't know why I'm telling you this. Not one other soul knows."

Karaleen grabbed her glass of water, and took several quick swallows, splashing some as she set the glass back on the table. What in the world made her confide in this man, a mere acquaintance?

Mr. Bradley reached across the table and placed his

149

hand on hers. "I didn't mean to pry," he said. "You'll have to forgive an old man's bumbling."

"No," Karaleen corrected, "I didn't have to blurt out all my private business. It's just that . . ." and for some unexplainable reason, Karaleen began to cry. She hid her face in a napkin and huddled in the booth, glad that they were in a dimly lit corner of the restaurant, and that the lunch crowd was gone.

Mr. Bradley waited, looking everywhere except at Karaleen.

After a few minutes, Karaleen composed herself and said softly, "It seems you've seen a side of me that not many others have. I haven't cried in public since I spilled a cherry cola on my white sweater at the fourth-grade picnic."

"Breaking an engagement must be a traumatic experience," Mr. Bradley said.

"Actually," Karaleen patted the napkin to her eyes, "it may not have been as traumatic as the telling of it. Lester and I should never have been engaged in the first place. My own father is so far away. I guess I needed to tell somebody."

She picked up her purse to go. "There. I believe I'm back together. I hope that I didn't completely destroy any idea you might have had of me as a competent business-woman."

Karaleen couldn't explain the tug on her heart as, back at the South County office, Mr. Bradley got into his rented car. Watching him drive away, she was overcome by a powerful sense of loneliness. It was as if she had known Arnold Bradley for weeks instead of hours.

She went into her office and closed the door. There on her desk was the silver pen he had used earlier making notes.

Karaleen rolled the pen back and forth between her fingers. She touched the smooth, cool metal to her cheek. It was then, as she tenderly cradled this tiny fragment of the Bradley family, that she knew she wanted desperately for this man's son to walk through the door and take her in his arms—knew she was deeply in love with Jason Bradley.

CHAPTER 10

THE NEXT WEEK LESTER came into Karaleen's office. "Harry tells me I have to get along without you for a few days."

Karaleen looked up in surprise. "What's this about?"

"He didn't explain, except that he needs you on a job at the home office. You're to catch a plane this afternoon. There's a meeting tomorrow that he wants you to attend."

"Why is Harry Turf always in such a hurry?"

Lester shrugged. "He's the boss. Bring me up to date on anything that can't wait until you get back."

The inhouse job of computerizing the South County office, could wait a little longer. "I've just about finished," Karaleen told Lester. "All I need is more work on the sales projection data."

At the San Francisco airport, Karaleen rented a car. She drove down the peninsula toward her apartment, finding it hard to stay within the speed limit. This was what she needed, she told herself, a bit of home to stabilize her feelings. How foolish she had been to fall in love with a man she would never see again. Somehow, she must shake the terrible longing for him that seemed to increase daily. Even if she were willing to give up her lifestyle, Jason had made it clear that any overtures on her part would be clearly viewed as gold-digging.

Arriving at her apartment, she threw open the windows to let the evening breeze blow through. It was almost too cool and damp for comfort, but Karaleen relished it and breathed deeply. She wished that she could exchange the emotions in her heart as easily as she could the air in her lungs.

By the next morning she had decided to insist that Harry transfer her back north. She hadn't belonged in South County when he first sent her, and she certainly didn't now. She desperately needed a fresh start.

At the office she made the rounds, greeting her co-workers. She hadn't realized how much she had missed everyone. Harry told her to catch up on her desk work and to be in his office at two o'clock for a meeting. When she attempted to pin him down about a re-assignment, he put her off. But she resolved not to leave Silicon Valley without a firm date for her return.

After an extended lunch hour with friends, Karaleen was in an exuberant mood as she walked into Harry's office at two o'clock.

Harry stood, an unusual practice for him during business hours. "Here's Karaleen now," he spoke to a man who sat in one of the two armchairs facing Harry's desk. The man also rose to meet Karaleen.

Karaleen's chest tightened. Her legs suddenly seemed unwilling to support her. Somehow she managed to nod at both the men and dropped into the chair Harry indicated. Of all the people in the world Karaleen expected to see at Vali-Turf, Jason Bradley was the last.

"How are you, Ms. Hammonds?" Jason inquired in

the same tone he might have used with a complete stranger.

"Fine, thank you," she heard herself answer politely. "And you?"

"Somewhat recovered since our last meeting," he answered.

Harry glanced from one to the other, an odd look on his face. "You two know each other, of course," he said by way of calling his meeting to order.

Just as Karaleen's pulse had quieted, and she was able to listen to Harry's conversation with Jason without using all her strength to keep her eyes away from the person in the dark business suit sitting so disturbingly close, she began to feel a new emotion—anger.

How dare Jason surprise her this way? Had he no compassion? Couldn't Harry have warned her? No, that wasn't fair to Harry. He didn't know what a fool she had been. What was Jason doing there anyway?

Harry shoved a sheet of paper toward her. It was something about shipping records. She forced herself to snap out of her daze.

When the meeting was over, Harry had agreed to a new job for AA-Bee Citrus that was far beyond the scope of the first. This one was more the size of Harry's usual projects.

"I'm sure you'll have the finest packing house operation in the state," Harry declared, "and certainly the most modern."

Jason shook hands with Harry. Then he turned and extended his hand to Karaleen. She inched hers forward until it was lost in his and held a little too long in a grasp a little too firm.

"We have confidence in the quality of your company's work," Jason told Harry, "and we're happy to have you and your people on the job," he indicated Karaleen. Her limp hand still lay within his. "I'll see you Monday, Ms. Hammonds, at the ranch."

Karaleen's head swam. As near as she could tell, Harry had committed Vali-Turf to a contract with Jason's citrus company to completely computerize a citrus packing house that was due to open in an unbelievably short time—with her name written into the contract as the programmer.

Jason was leaving. She must put a stop to such an unthinkable arrangement. No words came.

But Harry halted Jason with a jovial, "Wait a minute. We can't let you walk out of here without some sort of celebration, can we, Karaleen?"

Karaleen knew she did not answer, but Harry went on as if she had jumped in with a suggestion.

"Karaleen is at loose ends, being back in town for such a short time. You two go out and have a nice dinner on me." He looked sharply at Karaleen, just as he had several times during the afternoon. "Honestly, Jason, she's usually more fun than this. See if you can't snap her out of whatever is bothering her."

Her face burning, she and Jason were ushered from Harry's office with instructions that she take Jason to dinner at Fisherman's Wharf in the city.

She drove Jason in silence to her apartment. Inside, she waved toward the living room. "You can wait in there."

After changing into a tailored, dark brown dress, she pulled on a beige lightweight coat. She knew better than to go into San Francisco any time of the year without a coat. In fact, she was already shivering, although not from cold.

She came from the bedroom to find Jason staring out the front window. He turned to the coffee table and ran his fingers over the Bible she had left there. She had dusted it off the previous night and read a chapter, not wanting to break the one per night pattern she had developed.

Karaleen thought to let him freshen up, too. Clearing her throat for his attention, she motioned to the bedroom. "You can wash up if you want. The bathroom is through there." She plumped the throw pillows on the sofa and straightened pictures that were already straight.

Jason returned. "It's a nice apartment. I wondered what your home would be like."

Her tone was casual, "Please don't judge my housekeeping by the way the place looks now. I've been away so long the dirt has gotten out of hand."

"Looks fine. It's like you, you know. Modern, organized; yet here and there are homey touches and frills that are soft and sentimental. Oh, I don't mean it's all frivolous." He was nervous, too. "It's obvious that a serious person lives here." He pointed helplessly at the Bible.

"We should go." She started for the door.

"Karaleen."

"I'm famished. How about you?" She mustn't let him say anything personal. If ever he stepped across the line between them, she would do something stupid, like throw herself at him.

Quickly he went on, "I know we can't start over as if nothing had gone wrong, but—"

She finished for him, "No, I'm sure others have tried." She took a deep breath and sighed an elaborate, "So-o-o. What kind of fish are you going to have? You must eat fish at Fisherman's Wharf, even if you hate it." She rattled on, "Harry would be disappointed if I didn't show you San Francisco's famous landmark. Perhaps I should bring back an abalone shell in case he asks for proof—"

Jason broke in roughly, "You don't have to do this. Why don't I just be on my way now? They do have cabs this time of night in the famous Silicon Valley, don't they?"

Karaleen bit her lip. They were going to be working together. It was absolutely essential that she start behaving like a mature businesswoman. "Sorry about the prattle. I'm surprised you didn't gag me. Please, come to dinner. I'll try to be a good hostess."

Karaleen supposed that anyone watching her and Jason during the evening that followed would have taken them for two strangers having a polite dinner, perhaps fulfilling a business obligation, which is what they nearly were. Both were careful to limit the conversation to safe subjects, topics they might have gleaned from the morning paper. Personal remarks concerned only happenings in their lives prior to that day when Karaleen had car trouble on her way to the agricultural convention.

When the check came, Karaleen unobtrusively placed her credit card on the tray and hid her face, pretending to drink tea from an empty cup. Jason sketched squares on the soft white damask tablecloth with the tines of a fork.

It was still early when Karaleen stopped her rented car in front of Jason's hotel back in Silicon Valley. Jason rested his hand on the door handle, but made no move to get out.

She ran her fingers over the steering wheel. "I almost forgot to tell you—maybe you already know— I saw your father last week."

"Yes, he called briefly from Phoenix. Mentioned that you had lunch, but didn't say much more."

"He's such a gentleman." She thought of his understanding at her outburst of tears.

"I'll see him at home this weekend. After that, he and Mother will be off to the midwest. They're meeting friends for a riverboat cruise down the Mississippi."

"That's nice," Karaleen said weakly. *Please, don't touch me—just don't touch me,* she pleaded silently. Their one physical contact during the entire evening had been a brief moment when Jason had taken her arm as they came down the steps from the restaurant. The pressure through her coat had burned like a flame.

Jason raised the door handle. "I'll see you Monday." A second later, he was out of the car in a movement so nimble it seemed his voice still must catch up. He closed the door and leaned down so that his face was backlighted in the bright lights of the hotel. His words floated to her across the empty seat. "I haven't given up on us, Karaleen. I can't."

He walked into the bustling lobby, and disappeared.

Back in South County, with Jason's final words thundering in her ears, Karaleen was a different person. As she prepared for the trip to AA-Bee Citrus Ranch, the memory of his face as he had declared, *I haven't given up on us*, baited her with an elusive hope that perhaps their differences could yet be worked out.

Sensitive, caring Rosalie noticed as Karaleen packed. "Good trip up north?"

"The best!" Karaleen caught herself. "No, it wasn't exactly the best. It's just that . . . oh, Rosalie, I have to tell you or I'll burst."

"Tell me what?"

"That maybe, just maybe . . ." Karaleen twirled around the room clutching her hair dryer to her breast, stopping only when the dryer's cord whipped smartly against the dresser. She rubbed her fingertips apologetically over the dresser's finish and continued, "Just maybe there's hope."

"You have to be talking about your love life," Rosalie laughed.

"Oh, Rosalie," Karaleen sank to the bed, suddenly serious, "my head tells me it can never work, but my heart wants it to so badly." She answered Rosalie's puzzled expression, "Jason, the man I met at the ag convention?"

Rosalie nodded.

Karaleen told Rosalie a little of the recent events, explaining how only days before she had been convinced she would never see Jason again. Now she was going to the ranch to work. "I know there is too much to overcome. Our lifestyles are still poles apart. And," her voice dropped sadly, "will he believe me when I tell him I want him, not his money?"

Rosalie toyed with the edge of the bedspread. "What about your job?"

Karaleen drew a trembling breath. "I might . . . I could . . . oh, yes, I *could* give up my job if there were no other way."

"You love him that much?"

"Oh, Rosalie, I never knew love could be like this."

"Do you think he loves you?"

Karaleen answered softly, blinking back tears. "He might have once, if I had let him."

Rosalie put a sympathetic arm around Karaleen. "You said it yourself," she whispered, "there's hope."

Driving up to the ranch Monday morning, Karaleen's high-flying emotions insisted upon ignoring the cautious reminders telegraphed from her logical mind. Long before the first citrus groves came into view, Karaleen had, in her imagination, written scenario after scenario of romantic episodes. Jason and she dined by flickering candlelight on the patio. Hand in hand, they watched a glorious sunset from the foothills above the ranch. In the swing beneath the big tree with her head snuggled against his shoulder, they hid from the moonlight as he told her that somehow—someway—everything would work out and that he could not exist without her.

But when she came to his kiss—sweet, powerful— the car swerved until the tires left the pavement and the steering wheel shook so hard that Karaleen snapped out of her dreaming. She stopped at the first opportunity and strode into a restaurant, planting her feet firmly on the ground with every step. Only after a cup of strong coffee and a stern admonition to herself did she continue the drive.

Her return to the AA-Bee Citrus ranch brought the sense of a warm, comfortable homecoming that deepened her happiness and anticipation. The yard in front of the Bradley home was as neatly cared for as ever. The roses were in full bloom, a profusion of delicate pastels, made even more spectacular by strategically placed bushes of deep, dark red.

Genevieve explained that Jason was out but had left some papers for Karaleen on the desk in the office.

Karaleen brushed aside a flash of disappointment. As she unpacked and made herself at home in the bright green and white room she had come to think of as her own, she cautioned herself over and over, "He must make the first move."

Genevieve brought a sandwich and a cold drink into the office where Karaleen worked. Later Karaleen vaguely heard the clock in the front room strike two, then three. She took a break, gazing from the window. Beyond the immediate grounds hung a backdrop of dark citrus foliage. In the distance rose the silver propellers of a wind machine, gleaming in the early summer sun.

Karaleen had just returned to her seat when a familiar voice sounded behind her. She gripped the desk and restrained herself long enough to ensure her composure before she turned to see Jason. He was exactly as she had pictured him, excitingly handsome even in his work clothes. In deference to the warm weather, the material of his plaid shirt was light-weight. His jeans were slightly dusty and his boots scuffed.

Her eyes searched his face hungrily for a sign that all was well, that he had meant what he said about not giving up on them. But he had turned aside. She followed his look and only then realized that a third person was in the room and that Jason had just introduced him.

"Russell is the plant engineer," Jason was saying. "You two have a lot to discuss, so I'll leave you to your schedules and diagrams."

Open-mouthed, Karaleen watched Jason whirl and abruptly leave the room.

"Ms. Hammonds? May I call you Karaleen?"

Karaleen forced a nod to the blond, rather slight man that stood before her. He was neatly dressed in a knit pullover shirt and jeans. She judged him to be in his late thirties.

"A computerized packing house is new to me, too," he said companionably, as if she were uncomfortable over the project they were about to launch. He couldn't know that she was suffering from shock at the way Jason had all but ignored her.

He drew up a chair. "I thought we'd work out a schedule and sort of trade ideas this afternoon. My wife is expecting me home at five tonight. It's my son's birthday," he explained with obvious pleasure. "Tomorrow morning, I'll pick you up at eight, if that's not too early, and we'll go into town so you can see the actual facility. You'll be surprised at what Jason's done with an old fashioned warehouse."

Nothing could surprise Karaleen now. With supreme effort, she matched Russell's enthusiasm as they began. Before long, it was five o'clock, and he was gone.

On her own, Karaleen walked around the house, stretching her legs, and then went back to work. She tried not to think about Jason. Surely, he would burst into the room any minute and at least speak to her. It was clear now that she had blown his remark about not giving up on their relationship all out of proportion. But, couldn't they meet on an amicable business basis?

Sometime later, a gentle tap at the door made her heart leap. But it was Genevieve.

"Wouldn't you like your dinner on the patio?" she

smiled kindly. "You've worked many hours. It will be bedtime before you know it."

The sun was indeed low. "Yes," Karaleen said dully, "the patio would be fine."

"In about ten minutes?"

"Fine. Thank you," and Karaleen put away her things.

As Genevieve brought a tray to the patio table, she encouraged, "You make yourself at home. I'll be going back to my place soon. Leave the dishes on the kitchen counter. I'll do them tomorrow." As she stepped into the kitchen, she said, "There's a whole library of books in the master bedroom. Maybe you can find something to your liking."

Karaleen was touched by the woman's concern, even though it made her feel even more depressed to know that she was so obviously an object of pity.

Most of the dinner went down the garbage disposal, and Karaleen rinsed the dishes and loaded them into the dishwasher. She busied herself tidying up the already neat kitchen. She wandered aimlessly through the house, flinching as memory after memory of Jason greeted her. At last she hurried down the hall and shut herself in her room.

She rose long before her alarm sounded the next morning and was waiting for Russell when he arrived. There had been no sign of Jason.

Russell was a conscientious and undoubtedly competent plant engineer. He made no secret of his pride in having been assigned such responsibility in Jason's new operation. As he explained the physical remodeling of the old warehouse that AA-Bee Citrus had purchased, he filled Karaleen in on the timetable established for the opening of the new packing plant.

"I know it's a rush job, but we have to be ready for the first pick of the navel season," he explained. "Contracts are signed with the other growers in the area, and our marketing force is going strong."

162

Before the morning was over, Karaleen knew her way through the big barnlike structure as if she had helped in its construction. Russell was a good instructor. She visualized the oranges on their trip through, being washed, sorted, and packed. He pointed out where the bagging machines would stand, and showed Karaleen the framework for the conveyor belts that would carry fruit to be packed in cardboard cartons.

"This winter you'll get a chance to see it in operation," he promised.

She knew better. Her job would be finished long before then, and she would not be back.

Jason appeared at the packing house briefly. She saw him talking to a carpenter out on the loading platform. He approached her and Russell, saying, "Giving our programmer the grand tour, I see?" Shortly after, without having spoken a word directly to Karaleen, Jason departed.

That afternoon in the ranch office, Karaleen, feeling foolish and hurt, determined to cram days of work into as few hours as she was able. She set a furious pace. If at all possible, she would finish what was absolutely necessary and leave the Bradley house the following morning.

Her back ached, and her fingers cramped. She worked without a break, but more and more often, she was forced to stop. She closed her eyes and cupped her palms over them, trying to relax her facial muscles and rest her eyes in velvety black darkness. Once, as she sat thus, she heard a noise behind her. She jerked upright and turned, but saw no one, although she was almost sure that minutes later she heard Jason's voice nearby.

She accepted a dinner tray and a pot of coffee gratefully from Genevieve, along with the caution, "Goodness, honey, are you trying to do everything in one night?"

When Karaleen reached the point where her mind

simply would no longer function with any degree of accuracy, and she was satisfied that she could wind things up in a matter of hours, she quit. Thinking she was too tired to sleep, she wandered into the master bedroom and selected a book of classic short stories. She removed her shoes and stretched out on the living room couch, prepared to lose herself in a make-believe world.

Sometime later, she roused to find that the book had fallen to the floor, and somehow she had been covered with a light blanket. She looked around nervously. It gave her a creepy feeling to think of anyone finding her asleep. It must have been Genevieve. How like her. Except, Genevieve should have retired to her little house back of the kitchen long ago.

Wide awake now, Karaleen knew it would be a while before she could sleep again. A long walk in the cool night air sounded like a good idea.

She opened the front door. The rose garden was splendid by dark, its lighter-colored blossoms almost luminous. She headed down the circular drive. Near the road she stopped. How alone she was; how quiet were her surroundings. No cows and horses on this ranch; just serene, orderly acre after acre of trees.

She retraced her steps, leaving the drive before she reached the veranda and following a path that led along the side of the house where the swing hung amid the spreading walnut trees. She could go around the house to the patio.

The air was clean and cool. The trees ahead had a familiar look. Yes, there was the swing. The path branched. She followed it away from the swing, away from the house. She passed a building, perhaps a garage. She had never explored this part of the grounds.

Soon she found herself deep into the citrus grove that encircled the house. Just as she prepared to turn and go back, she saw a light ahead. Certain that there could be nothing to fear in this idyllic setting, she proceeded until she stood before a small cottage. A wide porch, only partially illuminated by light from curtained windows, ran across the front.

Not wanting to be thought spying by the ranch employee living there, Karaleen gingerly backed away. She had gone no more than a few steps, keeping watch on the front porch, when she suddenly stepped off the path. Her ankle gave way, she lost her balance, and, with a soft cry, fell to the ground.

She caught herself on her hands, wincing from the path's gravel that pricked at her palms. She gasped, first in pain, then in sudden, sharp fear as a form emerged from the shadows on the front porch. It bounded down the steps and rushed at her.

She wanted to scream, but she was paralyzed, unable to resist the strong arms that swooped her up into a grip of iron. The scream broke loose, and a rough hand clamped over her mouth. Karaleen struggled furiously, moaning through the hand.

A man's voice penetrated her panic, "Stop, Karaleen! It's me."

As the urgent words took on meaning, she sagged against Jason, sapped by fright. Gasping for breath, she tried to brush away the stinging gravel that clung to her hands, but Jason imprisoned her so that she could do little but submit to a torrent of questions.

"Are you hurt? Can you walk?" His concern was edged with roughness that matched the roughness in the hand that had clamped over her mouth. "What were you doing wandering around by yourself? I thought you were asleep for the night."

So he had covered her with the blanket so tenderly that she hadn't known he was there, the same person who, for the past two days, had rudely ignored her.

Confused by his lightning changes of personality, she concentrated on the physical feat of standing upright. Her legs steadied, but her heart refused to slow its mad pace. She must get away before Jason noticed, before he could read the trembling that was fast overcoming her. She could not bear for him to suspect the extent of her feelings toward him. Never would she give him reason to accuse her of fortune-hunting, and never again would she let herself hope for Jason's love—only to find he had once more turned on her.

She attempted to slip from his grasp, but Jason's hold was unyielding. He put one hand under her chin, his fingers pressed around her face, tilting it upward. He bent over her. She could feel his lips as if they already touched hers.

With all her strength she fought a powerful desire to surrender. She pushed at him uselessly. "Let me go," she cried. "Don't ever touch me again."

Jason's grip tightened, his fingers dug into her face. He forced his body close to hers.

Karaleen begged, the words barely audible, "Jason, let me go. I don't understand. You've never been like this. What's the matter with you?"

"What's the matter with me? I'll tell you what's the matter," his voice rang desperately. "I'm insane—insane for thinking I was in love with a woman who thought she was too good for a farmer, a woman who is only interested in me as a business partner."

His breath warmed her face. "Tell me, was it fun watching me? Did you enjoy seeing my clumsy efforts to control myself? To respect you and treat you like the Christian girl I'd waited for?"

"Please, I never. . . ."

He towered over her, crushing her to him. His lips came down on hers. His kiss was deep, thirsting. Karaleen was helpless. His embrace was like nothing she had ever felt—insistent, demanding. Even through the shock and fear of Jason's unbridled behavior, a wild urge to respond surfaced momentarily. She repressed it. Bewildered, spent, she went limp in this stranger's arms until at last he released her.

She drew the back of her hand across her face as if to wipe away the touch of his lips. She began to run, but with a single step, stumbled, crying at the pain in her ankle. Before she could fall, she was swept into Jason's arms. With swift, long strides, he carried her wordlessly back toward the main house.

Karaleen tried to read the look on his face, but the flickering shadows and her state of mind made it impossible. Her arms were clasped around his neck, and for the barest friction of a second, she wondered if, through some miracle, she had imagined their conflicts and that everything would be all right.

Jason stalked across the patio and over to the sliding door that led to her bedroom. Uttering an indistinguishable sound, he whipped away from the bedroom door, and marched to a chair on the patio. He left her there.

She heard the quick scrape of his boots across the patio as he vanished into the darkness.

CHAPTER 11

THE NEXT MORNING KARALEEN limped out of her bedroom and into the Bradleys' office. Only her respect for Harry and Vali-Turf prevented her from immediately escaping from the AA-Bee Citrus ranch back to civilization, flinging the work she had done from the car windows as she went. Instead she jammed everything into her briefcase. She would take it to the South County office. There, she would package it and ship it to Harry. He could get someone else to work for this unpredictable man.

From behind, Jason's voice caught her off-guard. "Russell called to say he'd been delayed for an hour or so."

She jumped, starting an avalanche of file folders. "I won't be here."

She felt the stinging sarcasm in his steely retort, "I'm perfectly aware that you're the top programmer in the Silicon Valley, *Ms*. Hammonds but don't tell me you're finished with even the preliminaries on this job."

She would stay calm; she would not show anger.

Unable to look Jason Bradley in the eyes, she hurled her defiant answer in his general direction. "I'm off this job, Mr. Bradley. But don't worry, Vali-Turf will give you your packing house system right on schedule."

Jason moved into the room, his stormy presence threatening Karaleen's composure. "I signed a contract with Vali-Turf. I expect that contract to be honored in every detail."

Karaleen threw her head back, ready to defend Harry's company. "Vali-Turf doesn't renege on its deals," she said proudly. "Harry runs an honest, ethical business. Everything's up front with him." She met Jason's hostile eyes and challenged. "It's too bad that everyone isn't as straightforward and dependable as Harry Turf."

"I couldn't agree more with that last statement," Jason snapped. "But it so happens that it is extremely important to me that this packing house go into operation on schedule. That's why I went to him when I decided to open a computerized facility. That's also why, Ms. Hammonds, since your name is written into that contract, you'll complete the work on time and to my satisfaction."

Karaleen clenched her fists. What reason could he have for doing this?

Jason continued, "I'm sure you don't want to drag Harry Turf into a nasty breach of contract situation. Lawsuits can be hard on one's reputation."

She would explain to Harry. Surely Harry could help. There must be a way that she wouldn't have to see Jason Bradley ever again. "Why do you care who does the programming? Harry can get somebody else."

"Perhaps, but, as I said, I want you." His eyes were cold, deliberately holding hers, sending a chill through her body. "You can do the job I need. This is strictly business. That is the kind of relationship you want, isn't it?" He waited, as if giving her the opportunity to contradict him. After an interminable moment, his lips parted in what could have passed for either a grin or a grimace. "Just consider this episode as another stepping stone in your career path."

He followed her to the car. She gritted her teeth and refused to favor her still painful ankle. With maddening casualness, he watched her pack her luggage and the leather briefcase in the trunk. Only a few seconds more and she would be safely away. The air was charged with angry emotion, but she must clear up one thing. "I put your father's silver pen in the top desk drawer. He left it in my office when he—"

"Yes, when he was here this weekend, he told me *all* about his visit to South County."

All about the visit? Jason wasn't making sense. None of this did. She slammed the trunk lid.

Then to her surprise, Jason raised his foot to the car's bumper and, with a powerful motion, scraped his boot across the bumper sticker that proclaimed *The Way*. As Karaleen scrambled into the car, she heard a muttered, "Hypocrite!" She sped away, more than ever at a loss to understand this monster who masqueraded as a Christian while he accused her of being a hypocrite.

Roaring down the road, she agonized, "How could I have let myself get involved with him?" She raced toward South County devoid of any thought of safety, intent on putting miles between her and Jason Bradley. "And I was even going to give up my job!"

In the weeks that followed, Karaleen resigned herself to working on the AA-Bee Citrus packing house system. She did little else, anxious to wind up the programming. After that someone else could complete the required on-site work. Surely Jason couldn't object to that.

Harry called and reported that Jason had been in contact with him about the job. "He seems satisfied with what we've done so far," Harry said. "I got the idea, though, that he feels we aren't taking enough personal interest in the work. Maybe you should take a run up that way, just to keep him happy?"

Karaleen wiggled out of it on the pretense that she could use the time to better advantage in the office. Harry had no compunction about tying up her weekends and when, on another occasion, he suggested she go up on a Saturday, she barely escaped by claiming a heavy social schedule for the weekend. "I'm on the phone to his plant engineer daily," she assured her boss, "and we're practically supporting the postal system."

During a brief visit to the South County office, Harry reviewed Karaleen's progress. In the middle of their conference, he asked, "Everything okay with you? You look pale."

"What I need is a little Southern California sunshine," she shot back, motioning through the office window to a day so bright the cartops reflected light like mirrors.

Lester, too, grew concerned over her health. "You and I are spending tomorrow on my friend's boat," he announced one Friday afternoon. "You've been working too hard." He looked her up and down. "Not eating enough either."

"Look who's talking about working too hard," she retorted. "I'm perfectly fine."

"Come on," Lester pleaded. "It'll be good for both of us."

She looked at him warily. "Lester," she paused, uncertain how to phrase her question.

He read her mind. "Just R-and-R. Honest." He spread his hands in a gesture of innocence.

Lying on the deck of a sleek thirty-foot sailboat on a calm, blue ocean, the warm sun soaking into her skin, Karaleen agreed that Lester's prescription had been precisely what she needed. His friend's boat was the

171

epitome of luxury, and she was in the mood to be pampered. She felt more relaxed than she had in weeks. The one tense moment throughout the long, lazy day came when she opened her sleepy eyes to find Lester staring at her as if he had some personal R-and-R in mind. She bolted upright and pulled a cover-up over her swimsuit.

Despite Rosalie and Rick's efforts to include her in their activities, Karaleen's social life was nearly nil. Being on temporary assignment, she couldn't shake the feeling of existing in a kind of limbo.

So Karaleen worked harder and faster. It helped keep her mind from dwelling on scenes that kept reappearing in her mind, on questions that surfaced repeatedly until she thought she might never be able to erase the memory of Jason Bradley.

She consented more and more often to dinner dates with Lester. They reached an unspoken agreement on a companionable relationship, although Karaleen often suspected Lester wanted to take up where they had left off before their engagement *un*announcement.

She, too, was tempted along those same lines. To thwart such inclinations, she worked more furiously on the AA-Bee Citrus system, determined that it would be her last job in the South County branch.

One day Karaleen reached an impasse in the packing house work. She was unable to get Russell on the phone to answer a question regarding the specs. So she picked up the inhouse computerizing work. Except for some input needed from Thelma, she was very close to completing it, and wanted badly to get it out of her hair.

As always, Thelma was uncooperative, but Karaleen dug through dusty files in the storeroom and came across copies of the annual reports done the previous two years. She doubted that anyone even knew they were there. Thelma's neat figures were impressive. In fact, the more Karaleen worked with the information, the more puzzled she became at how spectacularly bright the old sales forecasts looked.

"I don't understand it," she mused to herself, "something doesn't fit."

She decided to sleep on it, but to no avail. The next morning she studied everything, searching for mistakes in her own work. She was about to take the problem to Lester when she thought to explore one last possibility. Rummaging through the storeroom, she located dog-eared bundles of original monthly sales memos handwritten by the sales force.

She checked and rechecked, unable to believe her eyes. There it was! The figures on the original salesmen's memos did not agree with the ones transferred to the first of the data charts used to feed into the final sales projection report. It was so simple! A zero had been added here and there—just enough to inflate the final figures.

Someone had deliberately made the sales forecasts appear better than they were!

An hour later Karaleen had uncovered a pattern. The sales projections had been inflated for periods starting more than a year before. About six months later, a reverse procedure was initiated and followed until the projections were reduced to near normal. Because actual sales had increased dramatically in recent months, the overall sales forecasts now reflected a total volume that was fairly well in line with what it would have been if all had flowed naturally.

Such a thing could go unnoticed if the same person handled all the financial matters in an organization, and only if that person who tinkered with the sales figures could compensate by adjusting other records if needed. Actually, Karaleen reasoned, perhaps no adjustments to the actual bookkeeping records were ever needed. The sales projections were simply that, projections to be used to present a picture of the prospects of the South County branch, and what good prospects they seemed.

Karaleen rested her head in her hands. The mystery of Thelma's weeks of unreasonable behavior was solved. Thelma knew that sales information for the office was scheduled to be computerized, and feared, rightly so, that Karaleen's arrival brought its beginning. That meant the end of her manual and autonomous control in that area and possible discovery of her past indiscretions. Next would come other aspects of the office manager's job. No wonder Thelma tried to make Karaleen miserable enough to flee right back to the northern office.

Karaleen jumped up and paced around the room. Now it was her turn to make things miserable for Thelma. Giddy with the power at her disposal, Karaleen thought how best to use it. Should she call a meeting, maybe even with Harry there, and reveal her findings? Should she arrange to ask embarrassing, but seemingly innocent, questions of Thelma—in the presence of Harry and Lester, of course?

Her imagination ran amok, until, suddenly, it stumbled over a question. Why had Thelma risked her job to make the office look good? Or, had someone put her up to it? If so, that someone could be only one person. Karaleen shuddered and put the thought out of her mind. Of course, it had to be Thelma who both engineered the scheme and carried it out. Thelma alone. Karaleen locked the papers in her file cabinet and went home.

Lester called for Karaleen at seven. They drove down the coast to an elegant English restaurant famous for its roast beef and Yorkshire pudding. Lester was in high spirits, which, combined with a magnificent meal, became contagious. After the delicious main course, Karaleen hadn't cared for dessert, but Lester had urged her to try the trifle. Now she toyed with the dish in front of her and looked across

174

the table at the handsome blond man in the stunning gray suit, wanting the evening to last.

He tapped a spoon smartly against his water goblet and said grandly, "I called this meeting . . ."

"Silly," she accused, but loved the cheery feeling his jovial manner gave her.

"Silence," he ordered. "Have you no respect? You're about to hear an earth-shaking announcement."

Karaleen quipped, "Sales are up two thousand percent?" Immediately she regretted the slip. Even the word *sales* brought a shiver of foreboding. Lost in the delightful evening, she had forgotten her short-lived but wicked suspicion of that afternoon.

"Oh, nothing so inconsequential as sales," Lester reprimanded.

Before he could go on with his charade, Karaleen heard herself probing and hated herself for it, "I bet Harry wouldn't agree with that assessment. I bet he hangs on every sales projection as if it were fact instead of . . . instead of fiction." She nearly choked on the last word.

Lester put down his fork. "They are facts, and he does that. Luckily, our forecasts have always made him happy. Why do you think, my dear, that the South County branch is still in business?" Lester spoke as if revealing a secret. "You know, a year and a half ago, just after I came with the company, I wasn't sure I had made the right move. Oh, I knew taking over this office was a gamble, a gamble that I was willing to make. And it did pay off. Harry gave me six months to get the branch headed in an upward direction. It was dangerously near my deadline when the sales projections finally began to improve."

Karaleen shoved her dessert back. She fought an overpowering urge to be sick. "That was fortunate."

"I prefer to consider it the result of good management," Lester corrected. "Honestly, though, I'll

175

never understand it. I didn't think our sales warranted such a rosy picture at the time. Oh, they've been great since then. And," he laughed, "you know the saying? Figures never lie."

Relief flooded over Karaleen. She was grateful that Lester rambled on about her interruption of his big announcement while she adjusted to the revelation that the sales projections juggling had not been his idea. His response was too candid to be doubted.

Thelma alone was guilty. She would have known of Harry's threat to close the office. She knew everything that went on in the South County branch. With the offices closed, she would have been out of a job— not that Thelma needed the money; talk was that Thelma, with her diamond rings, was well-to-do. But Thelma might never find another position with the authority to run everything and everybody. And she probably reasoned that she wasn't stealing anything— just adjusting figures to create a sales picture with its indicators on a perpetual high.

"Hey, Karaleen," Lester prodded, "come back to this planet. Aren't you interested in my news?"

"Of course, I am, Lester. Sorry."

Pacified with Karaleen's undivided attention, Lester went on, "It's not Harry's sales I'm concerned with."

"Oh?" Something in Lester's tone alerted Karaleen that her dinner companion did after all have an important announcement.

Lester leaned toward her, his expression earnest. "I'm making a move, Karaleen."

"What do you mean?"

"It's a big move. The biggest." Lester looked around furtively. "I haven't told anyone else, but I've been negotiating a deal that has finally jelled." His eyes gleamed with excitement. He reached for her hand. "You're looking at the president of a new company."

An electrifying thrill raced from Lester's hand to hers. "That's . . . that's breath-taking," she whispered hoarsely. "Why, Lester, how wonderful for you. What? Where?"

"All the details aren't worked out yet, but I've got the backing, some tentative orders, and even the location."

"You said a new company?"

"That's right. It's a computer programming company. I've got funding to carry me for a year, thanks in part to my friend with the boat. The office space is leased." He winked at Karaleen. "Aren't you going to ask me where?"

"Where? Don't keep me in suspense."

"Where else? Silicon Valley."

Karaleen laughed. "Oh, no. I should have known it wouldn't be long before you'd be heading a company and, of course, you'd manage to be right up there with the big boys. That's great, Lester. I'm happy for you."

Lester's grip on her hand tightened. "Be happy for yourself, too."

Karaleen's throat was suddenly dry. She pulled her hand away and raised her goblet to her lips. With an effort, she sipped the cool liquid.

"I'm serious, Karaleen." Lester took the glass from her hand and faced her squarely. "I want you to come with me. You'll be Programming Manager. Don't you see? You'll be in on the start of a new, growing company. It's the perfect opportunity for you—for us."

Karaleen found her voice. "For us?" she repeated.

Lester withdrew slightly. "We'll keep it purely business if that's the way you want it."

She avoided his gaze, knowing what was coming next.

"However, this arrangement can go as far as you choose, Karaleen. It's your option."

Karaleen's mind whirled. A chance to get back to Silicon Valley, to be the Programming Manager in a new company. What more could she ask? It would mean leaving Vali-Turf, but hers was an ever-changing profession, and a move to better one's position was the accepted thing. Harry would understand that.

Except, she looked past Lester's animated face to the eager, expectant gleam in his eyes. Well, never mind that. Lester had just promised they could keep it on a business level unless she chose otherwise. She could decide that later.

"What do you think, honey?"

She ignored the endearment. "Lester, this is too much for me to digest." She sighed and smiled at him, "Especially after that meal. Give me some time."

"Sure. Take some time."

When he left her at the apartment door, she kissed him lightly on the cheek. "Lester, I'm terribly happy for you."

"I'll have to tell Harry soon," Lester said. "Don't keep me up in the air long."

Inside Karaleen realized she knew almost nothing about the company itself. Lester said no one else had been told. That must mean he didn't have a staff lined up. What specific services would it offer? Now that her head was clearing, she thought of so much that she wished she had asked.

The next morning Lester came into her office and shut the door. He sat in the visitor's chair opposite her desk. "What do you think?"

She knew exactly what he meant, but stalled, "About what?"

He laughed nervously, "The weather, of course."

She smiled back. "There's a lot I need to know." She lowered her voice. "I haven't heard anything about the organization set-up. How large an operation is it? Does it involve hardware? What market are you aiming for?" She shrugged, "Maybe my capabilities won't parallel your customers' needs."

178

Lester smirked, "Let me be the judge of that." But he drummed his fingers against the arm of his chair, a rare practice for him.

"Specifically," she pursued, "what kind of work are you going to do?"

Lester shifted, crossing an ankle over his knee. He rubbed his face with one hand. "Your kind of work," he blurted out.

Karaleen must have shown her astonishment.

He rushed on, "It's right in line with your experience. The fit couldn't be better."

A hard knot began to form in the pit of her stomach.

Lester ran a hand through his hair. "We'll be aiming for the agriculture market. Harry was right. There's a wide-open field out there," a loose-lipped smile spread across Lester's face, "if you'll pardon the pun."

The knot in Karaleen's stomach grew into a rolling, lurching ball. She held up her hands. "I don't want anything to do with farmers!"

"Hey, now, farming is big business. I know some other industries may seem more glamorous; however, it's a trade-off. You get less glamour, but the potential in agriculture is immense. Why, we'll be sitting pretty after just this first packing house." Lester stopped short, then hurried on, "You know yourself, how much gross there is in computerizing one packing house, and there are—"

Karaleen heard a voice that came from somewhere. It couldn't have been hers; she had just been rendered totally numb. "Citrus packing house?"

"For a start. But, don't forget about almonds, and—"

"Lester," she knew it was her voice this time because each word hurt as she squeezed it out, "you said you had tentative orders. Do you have an order for a packing house job?"

Tiny beads of perspiration gathered on Lester's brow. "It's tentative. I told you that."

"What will it take to make it final?"

"Some details. Some details have to be worked out."

Karaleen half rose from her chair. "Details like guaranteeing a programmer who's already done another packing house job? Or, maybe a programmer who quits on the other packing house job before it's finished? That sort of thing could slow the competition, you know."

Lester's lips clamped in a thin line.

Her mind raced. "Maybe," she ventured, "maybe the funding for the company itself is contingent upon leaving Harry and AA-Bee Citrus in the lurch. Maybe there won't be any company for you to be president of until you can come up with a computer system for this customer."

Lester jumped to the defense, "Now, Karaleen, that isn't so. You're not the only programmer who could do the job I need. I'll admit, you have a headstart." He was once again the vigorous executive speaking, "Remember, Karaleen, this would be good for you as well as for me. You're always talking career growth. Think about that before you pass up this opportunity."

The rest of the week it was almost impossible for Karaleen to think of anything else. Trying to be methodical and organized, she outlined the pros and cons of the decision and reviewed them again and again.

If she took Lester's offer, it would be her chance to return to Silicon Valley. Lester would no doubt go far; why not use him to advance her own career, just as he proposed to use her? And even if Lester's company never got off the ground, holding the title of Programming Manager in any organization would look good on her resume.

There would be one plus in accepting Lester's offer

which Karaleen didn't list as she ticked off the others. It was hidden away where she did not have to face it, but she knew it was there because it kept urging, *Go ahead. Go ahead. Jason Bradley deserves to be hurt. He hurt you, didn't he?*

A negative aspect of joining Lester's company, however, bothered Karaleen enormously. Leaving Jason's job unfinished and walking out with the considerable knowledge she had gained in how to put together the packing house program would be a disservice to Harry Turf. Sure, the program was only one of many for Vali-Turf, but she did not want to harm Harry even a little.

There was something else, too. Ethics. But who was to decide which ethics were valid in the fast-paced competitive race to get ahead?

At night Karaleen couldn't sleep. During the day she couldn't rest, driving herself with a compulsion to complete work, to put everything behind her.

Late Friday afternoon, the day before Rosalie and Rick's wedding, Karaleen did finish the essential work on the AA-Bee Citrus packing house job. Now it was ready to turn over to Harry. Quietly she locked the material in her file cabinet and went to the apartment, determined to think of nothing the next twenty-four hours except her friends' wedding.

The ceremony was beautiful in its simplicity. Through misty eyes, Karaleen saw love in Rick's every look, every movement, as he took Rosalie for his wife. She wondered if she would ever, like Rosalie, marry a man who treasured her, a man who wanted to care for her for the rest of his earthly life, and who invited God to share their home.

Lester had been asked to the wedding weeks before as Karaleen's guest. During the reception in the garden adjacent to the chapel, he whispered, "Have an answer for me yet?"

"Soon," she promised.

That night the apartment was so lonely that Karaleen could hardly stand it. Rosalie's furniture had been moved to her new home, leaving only that belonging to her roommate away on the work assignment. Karaleen wandered about, feeling lost. "Face it," she scolded herself, "it's not the scarcity of furniture that makes this place a morgue. It's you. You're dead."

Her own words, spoken aloud, shocked Karaleen. She was getting downright morbid.

The next day she went to church, thinking of Rosalie and Rick honeymooning in Santa Barbara. After church she was pleased that several people invited her to join them for lunch. But she begged off and drove to the spot of beach she had come to know so well.

Karaleen left her shoes and stockings in the car. She walked along the shore as fast as she could, not caring that the skirt of her thin white dress was wet from the splash of the surf, or that her legs grew raw from the sand that rubbed against them as the wind whipped the dress about her. At last, exhausted, she dropped to the beach. She put her head on her knees and cried.

God, she said, *I've always thought I was a Christian, and I always tried to act the way I supposed a Christian should. But it seems that merely living a good life doesn't make me a Christian.* Rosalie had insisted that being a Christian meant believing that Jesus was—and is—God, and that a Christian must make a deliberate choice to depend on Him, to follow Him, forever more.

Karaleen looked up and, brushing back strands of limp dark hair, gazed out over the ocean. *God, I choose Jesus. I'm accepting Him as Your son.* A breeze caught her words and whisked them away. *I want to be a real Christian. I'm handing my life over to You.*

After a while she rose and started back along the beach, the waves lapping gently at her feet.

On Monday morning Karaleen arrived early at the South County office. To her surprise, the outside door was already unlocked.

She went down the empty hall to her office. There she was surprised to find Harry waiting in her visitor's chair. To her further amazement, he sat unmoving, staring out the window, instead of, as usual, busily shuffling papers or scribbling notes.

He greeted her first. "You look terrible."

She supposed she did, but she wished she didn't have to hear about it. "Thanks," she answered glumly. She placed her briefcase on the credenza and seated herself at her desk.

Something big was bothering Harry. She hated to add to his burden, but her decision had been made.

"I have two things for you," she began. She unlocked the file cabinet and pulled out a stack of file folders and a book of bound printouts. The labels with their notations of "Packing House" were smeared and worn to the point of being almost unreadable, but Karaleen experienced a sense of satisfaction at the contents as she gave them to Harry. He placed them on the corner of her desk with barely a glance at the labels.

Next she removed a plain white envelope from her purse. Brushing aside a last-minute misgiving, she handed it to Harry.

He turned it over and over in his hands. "You're sure about this?"

It was as if he knew what was inside, as if he was already disappointed at her resignation.

"You don't even know what it is," she accused, trying unsuccessfully for a light tone.

Harry gave her a look that claimed he could read her every thought; certainly he could decipher anything as transparent as a paper envelope. "I suppose you've given me a generous two-weeks' notice?" he asked.

"How did you know?" she demanded.

With no hint of pleasure at his insight, he told her, "You're talking to the fellow who keeps tabs on his company and his employees. Remember?"

Karaleen would miss Harry.

He slipped a sheet of paper from the white envelope and unfolded it, his eyes scanning her hand-written resignation.

In a rush of affection, she blurted out, "Harry you know you've been more than a boss to me. I hope I can find another like you. I'm counting on you to give me a good recommendation when I start looking for a new job."

Harry leaned forward in the chair as if the wind had been knocked out of him. His face paled. "Come off it, Karaleen. Don't play that kind of game. It's bad enough that you're stabbing me in the back. Let's be honest. You know exactly what you're doing. You're running out on me, leaving a job half-done, and setting yourself up in competition."

The room tilted and swirled, becoming one undulating background from which Harry's disappointed, accusing face stood out sharply. It frightened her; yet she focused on it, trying to keep herself from slipping into the surrounding murky shadows.

"Wait, Harry!" she cried. "You've got it wrong. I'm not running out on you. I'm not competing with anybody." What was he talking about? Why, Harry sounded as if she were a part of Lester's scheme! But, Harry didn't even know about Lester's plans to form a new company.

If only she could explain to Harry that she was leaving so she would be safely situated in a new unrelated job when Lester started his venture. If only she could tell him that she was resigning so there would be no question of her aiding Lester's competitive efforts. She could not supply proprietary information to Lester when she was neither a Vali-Turf employee nor connected with Lester's new company.

"I just have to make a major change," she said weakly.

"You're right," Harry barked. "You have to make a major change."

Karaleen recoiled at Harry's sharp tone and stared in open disbelief at his next words.

"I want you to clean out your desk, Karaleen—*now!*"

CHAPTER 12

A FORM APPEARED IN the inner doorway between Karaleen's and Lester's offices. Instantly Harry was on his feet, moving in that direction, leaving Karaleen to fend off a feeling of faintness that was fast closing in.

She had been fired from her job! Harry had *fired* her.

An angry dialogue erupted from Lester's office.

"There's nothing wrong with a good clean break," Harry was saying, "but this is dirt. If I can't salvage the citrus job, I'll be liable for damages on that contract."

"It was that snooping Thelma, wasn't it?" Lester's voice soared through the building. "She told you."

A flurry of traffic sifted into the hallway. Thelma's thin figure appeared.

"Her little hint started my investigation," Harry agreed, "but she made a big mistake. She assumed that Karaleen, being the programmer on the packing house contract, was the only person involved in this espionage deal. I'm sure Thelma had no idea I'd discover a conspiracy with you leading it."

Lester laughed harshly. "Joke's on Thelma. I was planning to give her a spot on my staff."

Numbly, Karaleen straightened her desk blotter and replaced a stray paper clip in its holder.

The employees in the hall disappeared with the exception of a solitary, thin figure, nervously fingering heavy diamond rings.

Karaleen got to her feet. She would clean out her desk as Harry had ordered. She opened a drawer, looked in it blankly, then closed it.

Lester appeared in her office. Harry followed and posted himself nearby, like a sergeant-at-arms.

"Karaleen, it seems my timetable has been upset." Lester was once again smooth-spoken, in control. "But that's not an insurmountable problem by any means." His eyes fell on the packing house material still on the desk where Harry had left it. Casually Lester sidled to the credenza and snapped open Karaleen's leather briefcase. He addressed Karaleen, each word replete with meaning, "Don't leave *anything* behind."

Harry, ever perceptive, moved to the desk and picked up the AA-Bee Citrus papers.

Karaleen stared at the two people so important in her life. Only one other man was more important. And just as she had discovered her love for Jason Bradley, he had abruptly switched whatever feelings he might have had for her into scathing, spiteful rejection.

Now she had no Jason and no job. But Lester was offering her one last chance to come with him.

Perhaps even now she could retrieve the AA-Bee Citrus material from Harry under some pretense. To delay the opening of the packing house would be just what Jason deserved. Regardless, she could still have the job with Lester. With him the career possibilities were unlimited. Marriage? Maybe someday. Would Lester consider becoming a Christian? He had as much as said so.

However, the temptation to build a new career on a unscrupulous foundation was short-lived. There was no doubt in Karaleen's mind what she must do. "Lester, I'm not coming with you. I've finished work on the packing house job and already given all of it to Harry. Yes, *all* of it." She heard Harry's quick intake of breath. "Another Vali-Turf employee can easily fulfill the on-site obligation." Harry lifted his face to look at her. Surprise was in his eyes.

Lester's face went white. He groped for words, sputtered unintelligibly, and finally eeked out, "Why?"

"Ethics, Lester. Ethics."

Lester cursed, his face twisted in anger. "Ethics! Don't give me that. This sort of thing is done every day. Who's to say what's ethical and what's not?"

Karaleen replied softly, "God." The room was deathly still. She might as well say it all. "I've decided to trust Him with my life. It seems reasonable to go along with His standards."

Never before had Karaleen seen Lester in defeat. A strange, almost wistful smile spread over his face, as if he longed to understand. Or was he simply thinking of what could have been? Silently, he backed through the doorway into his office, his athletic body seeming to dematerialize as if he were merely some shadowy figment in this unbelievable nightmare.

Karaleen's knees folded and she sank into her chair.

Harry indicated the AA-Bee Citrus material, his eyes strangely bright. "So this is all of it? And you weren't resigning to join Lester's company, were you?"

She shook her head.

"And I brag about being able to judge people," he chided himself. "I'm so sorry, Karaleen. I should have gone with my gut feeling about you. Come back to the home office with me. I'll have somebody down here this afternoon to start phasing out this branch."

She shook her head. "I can't, Harry. I need a new start."

Left alone, it took only a short time for Karaleen to pack her few personal items in the leather briefcase. She went through the files quickly, labeling and sorting for those who would take over when the material arrived at the home office.

At the sight of the inhouse computerizing job, Karaleen caught her breath. Now was her chance to get even with Thelma by telling Harry about the office manager's false sales projections. First she would confront Thelma.

Taking the old sales memos with their altered figures and the inaccurate sales projections data, she marched into Thelma's office and slammed them on the desk. Thelma twitched in her usual skittish manner and then grew still, her eyes lowered behind her oversized glasses, a glint from the designer frames bringing the only sign of life to her expressionless face. About thirty seconds would be needed for Thelma to get Karaleen's message.

But during that span of thirty seconds, Karaleen suddenly realized to her own astonishment that she no longer wanted revenge on Thelma.

Snatching a red pencil from Thelma's desk, Karaleen scrawled across the top of the telltale evidence, *Obsolete—to be destroyed.*

A shiver, barely perceptible beneath Thelma's tailored silk blouse, served as her only acknowledgment.

A few minutes later, Karaleen walked out of Vali-Turf's South County office. She turned her face up to the bright Southern California sun. *God*, she sighed, *"I don't know what's next, but You're in charge."*

She drove to the apartment, and by late afternoon, had it in good order. There was no reason to stay longer in South County. She wrote a brief note for Rosalie's roommate, who was due to return soon.

Karaleen would pack her car and start home. She could stop for the night along the way. The quicker she got back on Silicon Valley soil, the better off she would be.

Karaleen showered and dressed in an open weave white blouse and salmon-colored slacks she had kept out for the trip north. She did a brief make-up job and tossed a lightweight beige sweater over her arm. As she carried the last suitcase out a knock sounded at the front door.

Harry stood there, a small bag at his feet and briefcase in his hand. He eyed Karaleen's suitcase, then signaled toward the street to dismiss his waiting taxi.

"I thought you might be leaving," he said.

Karaleen was struck dumb by the appearance on her doorstep of her former boss. She stood, awkwardly twisting her sweater and trying to think of something to say.

Harry spoke up, "Got room for a passenger?"

"You want to ride to the Bay Area with me?"

"Is that so strange? A fellow gets tired of flying. You get more of a feel for the countryside when you're in it, instead of over it. Besides, I'm going in for this ag stuff in a heavy way. Need to look over some of my territory.

"I'll drive," he said as they got into her car. "You look terrible."

"You keep telling me that," she complained.

They stopped for a light supper. Harry tried valiantly to cheer her, and she appreciated his effort, even though it was singularly unsuccessful. She offered to drive as they left the restaurant, but he motioned her to the other side of the car.

On the road again, he broached the subject of her work. "You know, Karaleen, there's no reason for you to leave Vali-Turf. Perhaps you could pull your horns in a little. Maybe you've gone at this ladder-climbing too hard."

190

She snorted. "If I were really serious about climbing the corporate ladder, I'd be programming manager for Lester's company right now, instead of out of a job."

"I mean, before all this. I think you need a change."

"That's what I said. I need a change." She was tired and getting drowsy. She snuggled down and draped her sweater across her chest like a blanket.

"We could work something out so you could do consulting, maybe act as our rep to the ag people. You could even move out in the country."

Karaleen squirmed, trying to stay awake. "Ag people? No thanks," she mumbled. "The last thing I want to see is a farmer. Temperamental . . ." Tears slid from beneath her closed lids. She pulled the sweater higher and turned her face from Harry.

Sometime later, Karaleen felt the car ease to a stop. She shifted in her seat and asked in a sleepy voice, "Where are we?"

"I have to deliver some papers. Sit tight."

She stirred. It was dusk. They should look for a motel soon. Surely Harry hadn't decided to drive on in. "What papers?"

Harry was climbing out. "It'll only take a minute."

Suddenly the scene outside the car jumped into focus. Karaleen jerked upright and cried, "Harry! What have you done?"

"Don't get excited. There were bound to be rumors about trouble at the South County branch, so I called your customer this afternoon. Promised him I'd get this stuff up here today." He pulled his briefcase from the back seat. "It was on our way home. You might as well come in. Looks like a snazzy house."

Karaleen was well acquainted with the "snazzy" house Harry referred to. How many times had she unsuccessfully tried to forget every moment spent in that beautiful Spanish home? She scooted down in the seat. "Harry, I can't come in. I don't want to see . . . I mean, I'm not your employee anymore."

"Oh, don't try to keep secrets from me. I know who you're hiding from. I had a long talk with Arnold Bradley this afternoon." Harry's voice was gruff. "I have a good idea of what's been going on between you and Jason Bradley. And if you want my opinion—"

"Harry! Shh."

"Okay. Nevertheless, business is business, and I'm delivering this. You can sit here, or do as you please."

"Harry," she pleaded, "don't tell anybody I'm here," but he was already stepping onto the veranda.

The heavy wooden front door opened, and closed.

Karaleen looked around. She saw no one. However, she could hardly feel more conspicuous, sitting in a car in the driveway.

She eased the door open. She would wait in a less visible spot, under the walnut trees in the side yard. She could listen for Harry. Hopefully he would return to the car soon and alone. How could Harry have brought her here? After talking to Arnold Bradley, he must know how upsetting it would be. Maybe he had even talked to Jason. Of course, Jason wouldn't care; she was only a business contact to him.

Through the lengthening shadows, she caught sight of the old swing and swallowed a lump in her throat. This place was filled with memories. Her eyes sought the tree where Jason stood that first night when he found her alone on the swing. She pictured him there, eager, restrained. He had wanted to take her in his arms then. She was certain of it. And she had wanted him to. What had happened between them since that night so long ago?

She went to the swing and rocked back and forth, the soothing motion relieving some of her tension. But its soft creak might give her away. She dragged her feet to stop.

Into the silence came a new sound. Footsteps. Someone was walking along the gravel path from the front of the house. It mustn't be Jason. In panic, she looked for a place to flee. But running would only draw attention. She would chance staying in the shadows of the overhanging tree.

She knew well where the gravel path led. Her heart pounded at the memory of Jason's crushing embrace that night she had wandered to his bungalow.

The heavy sound of boots came closer, then stopped. She shivered although the air was warm. Had the wearer paused, or had he left the path? Was he even now crossing the soft grass in her direction?

She waited in turmoil. She wanted, and yet dreaded to see the tall form that appeared, striding swiftly toward her. She knew instantly that it was Jason. Escape was impossible. If only she could hide her futile feelings.

He stopped just short of the swing, and held out his hand. She shrank as if he might strike her.

He moved closer. Something glowed in his open palm.

A single pink rose.

Karaleen gasped. Tears welled up and overflowed. Maybe he wouldn't be able to see them in the near-dark. She fought to control the sobs that threatened to engulf her. She made no move to accept the flower.

Jason gently placed the rose across her hands. After a bit she raised it to her face, automatically inhaling the faint fragrance. She twirled the stem between her fingers. A thorn pierced her skin. She dropped the flower, her finger flying to her mouth with the taste of blood.

"No, no, no!" she cried, half pleading, half demanding. "Don't do it again. You've no right to let me think . . . being sweet and gentle one minute, and hateful the next." She turned aside, grasping the swing's chain with both hands and burying her face against her arms. "Go away. You're not going to hurt me again."

"I've talked to Harry." Jason spaced his words as if it were an effort to speak calmly. "I learned a few things I should have found out for myself a long time ago."

"Leave me alone," Karaleen begged.

He sat beside her. She shrank from him, widening the space between them.

"Karaleen, I know I've been what you said— hateful. And worse, I was a hypocrite, at the very moment I was accusing you of being one."

He rocked the swing gently. "You see, I was impatient for God to give me the right person in marriage, and when you came along, I was sure you were the one. I set out to prove to you that a farmer's life wasn't all bad. Then, when I found you didn't want to marry a hick farmer, I thought I'd let you know that I was a boss, not the hired hand. I'd show you I could be as ruthless and as sophisticated as—"

"Don't, Jason, please," Karaleen whispered, cringing at the thought of that humiliating scene with his parents.

"But I couldn't give up. That's why I insisted that you work on our packing house. I was still sure that you were the Christian girl for me. Even my father was captivated by you. After his visit to your office, he warned me that I'd better move quickly and grab you before someone else did. He didn't know how hard I'd already tried to grab you." A bitter laugh bubbled from Jason's throat. "Then he told me about your engagement. That was how I discovered that, all the time I was making a fool of myself over you, you were engaged to someone else."

Karaleen turned to face him. "Stop! Don't you think I've gone over that a thousand times?"

But Jason raced on, "In my anger, I told myself no Christian girl would treat me that way. So I labeled you a hypocrite and lashed out at you in every way I could. That night over by the cottage, I treated you the way I thought . . ." His voice broke, "the way I thought you'd expect." He buried his head in his hands. "No," he admitted hoarsely, turning from her, "it was more than that; it was the way I felt. Right then, I did exactly what I desired, what *I* wanted to do at that moment. I was as much a hypocrite as I told myself you were."

Karaleen rested her head against Jason's back, and hugged him as if to comfort a child. How he must have been tormented, believing from the first day they met that she was a Christian. How he must have puzzled over her values and ached over the wisdom of his feelings for her, the same way she had wrestled with them and with her relationship with Lester.

"Oh, Jason," she cried, "don't you see? I couldn't tell you about the engagement because . . . because the telling would have made it real . . . and it never was."

Jason shuddered, the tenseness in his shoulders easing slightly.

Karaleen rushed on, "You had good reason to wonder about my Christian principles—not in the way you thought—but that's changed now."

Jason said sadly, "I was supposed to know where I stood in my Christian life. I was too smitten with you—too in love—to think of offering my help." Karaleen pulled away, her hands in her lap. Beside her, Jason straightened, and began idly pushing the swing.

"Even if . . ." Jason said, almost to himself. The swing hummed its little song. "I'm still a farmer."

"Yes," Karaleen sighed. Jason's arm dropped across the back of the swing. Although it didn't touch her, she could almost feel it through the open weave of her blouse.

They rocked gently. Karaleen said hesitantly, "I

didn't think I could ever marry a farmer until . . ." her voice trailed off.

The swing stopped abruptly. "Until?"

Karaleen's own whispered words thundered in her ears. "Until I fell in love with one."

Jason's hand crossed the invisible barrier between them, catching her shoulder in a powerful grip.

"I resisted as long as I could," she confessed, her voice breaking. She finished helplessly, "Then it was too late."

The barrier fell completely. Jason folded her into his arms. "It's not too late," he insisted, stroking her hair feverishly and pressing her face against his chest. "Don't say its too late."

Overcome with joy at his embrace, Karaleen fought down the blind hope that threatened to gloss over a yet unresolved question.

"Darling," Jason's voice was husky, "I love you more than I can begin to tell you. It's right. It has to be. Somehow we must make it work. I know there's still your—"

"My career? My other love?"

He said nothing, but leaned back against the swing, one hand caressing the nape of her neck.

She forced a laugh. "Well, as of this morning, I happen to be unemployed."

"I heard," Jason said quietly. He drew her hand to his lips, kissing her fingers one by one until he pressed her hand to his cheek with a fierceness that belied his gentle offer, "I have a job for you."

Karaleen longed to give in, to forget this last obstacle. "If I accept your job offer," she began cautiously, "suppose I did. First, how would you know whether I wanted you or . . . or all this?" She gestured around them. "Second, would you always wonder if I could have brought myself to quit a good job and abandon my career for marriage?"

"Forever the methodical programmer, aren't you? The real question is, would *you* know, Karaleen?"

She had already reached her decision that night in Rosalie's apartment when she had realized that Jason was more important than her cherished career. "I'd know," she answered firmly.

"Then, so would I." But to her surprise, he chuckled, "Funny thing, though, I didn't hear any proposal of marriage? Aren't we talking about a job computerizing—?"

Karaleen gasped and twisted away.

He laughed and pulled her to him. "Harry did say that he had offered you a job you could handle when I give you time off from tending the rose bed in front of this house. It sounded as if you'd be able to work right out of that fancy briefcase of yours, with maybe a call here and there." Jason released her slightly to ask, "Would that be enough for you, Karaleen?"

She nodded, savoring the touch of his lips against her forehead before she straightened and asked mischievously, "And what makes you think I'd be tending your roses?"

"Because, I'm asking you to marry me. They'll be your roses, too." Suddenly serious, he cupped her face in his hand, and gently ran his fingers over her cheek, along her throat. "I want us to be husband and wife. Don't you see, Karaleen? You are the one God has sent to me."

Karaleen returned his look of pure love. "I know, Jason. If not, I could never feel this way." Her arms stole around his neck.

His kiss was tender and patient and loving.

ABOUT THE AUTHOR

MARY CARPENTER REID is a writer from Brea, California. She and her husband have three grown children—Mary, Caren, and Daniel. Mary and Howard own an orange grove in Central California, for which she does the bookkeeping. Mary also enjoys writing and editing on her computer at home.

A Letter to Our Readers

Dear Reader:

Welcome to the world of Serenade Books—a series designed to bring you the most beautiful love stories in the world of inspirational romance. They will uplift you, encourage you, and provide hours of wholesome entertainment, so thousands of readers have testified. In order that we might better contribute to your reading enjoyment, we would appreciate your taking a few minutes to respond to the following questions and return to:

> Editor, Serenade Books
> The Zondervan Publishing House
> 1415 Lake Drive, S.E.
> Grand Rapids, Michigan 49506

1. Did you enjoy reading KARALEEN?

   ☐ Very much. I would like to see more books by this author!
   ☐ Moderately
   ☐ I would have enjoyed it more if _____

   _____

2. Where did you purchase this book? _____

3. What influenced your decision to purchase this book?

   ☐ Cover   ☐ Back cover copy
   ☐ Title   ☐ Friends
   ☐ Publicity   ☐ Other _____

4. What are some inspirational themes you would like to see treated in future books?

_____

5. Please indicate your age range:
   ☐ Under 18   ☐ 25-34   ☐ 46-55
   ☐ 18-24   ☐ 35-45   ☐ Over 55

6. If you are interested in receiving information about our Serenade Home Reader Service, in which you will be offered new and exciting novels on a regular basis, please give us your name and address. (This does NOT obligate you for membership.)

Name _____

Occupation _____

Address _____

City _____ State _____ Zip _____